WEDDING NIGHT WITH HER ENEMY

BY
MELANIE MILBURNE

First Published in Great Britain 2017
By Mills & Boon, an imprint of HarperCollins*Publishers*
1 London Bridge Street, London, SE1 9GF

© 2017 Melanie Milburne

ISBN: 978-0-263-92448-0

Printed and bound in Spain
by CPI, Barcelona

Melanie Milburne read her first Mills & Boon at the age of seventeen, in between studying for her final exams. After completing a Master's Degree in Education she decided to write a novel—and thus her career as a romance author was born. Melanie is an ambassador for the Australian Childhood Foundation and a keen dog lover and trainer. She enjoys long walks in the Tasmanian bush. In 2015 Melanie won the HOLT Medallion—a prestigious award honouring outstanding literary talent.

Books by Melanie Milburne

Mills & Boon Modern Romance

The Temporary Mrs Marchetti
Unwrapping His Convenient Fiancée
His Mistress for a Week
At No Man's Command
His Final Bargain
Uncovering the Silveri Secret

The Ravensdale Scandals

Ravensdale's Defiant Captive
Awakening the Ravensdale Heiress
Engaged to Her Ravensdale Enemy
The Most Scandalous Ravensdale

The Playboys of Argentina

The Valquez Bride
The Valquez Seduction

Those Scandalous Caffarellis

Never Say No to a Caffarelli
Never Underestimate a Caffarelli
Never Gamble with a Caffarelli

Visit the Author Profile page at millsandboon.co.uk for more titles.

To Laura Melania Kacsinta Bernal.
Thanks for being such a lovely fan.
This one is for you! Xx

CHAPTER ONE

ALLEGRA KALLAS WASN'T expecting a fatted calf or a rolled-out red carpet and a brass band. She was used to coming home to Santorini with little or no fanfare. What she expected was her father's usual indifference. His polite but feigned interest in her work in London as a family lawyer and his pained expression when she informed him that, yes, currently she was still single. A situation for a Greek father of a daughter aged thirty-one that was akin to having a noxious disease for which there was no known cure.

Which made her wonder why there was a bottle of champagne waiting on a bed of ice in an ice-bucket with the Kallas coat of arms engraved on it and a silver tray with three crystal glasses standing nearby, and why he was gushing about how wonderful it was to have her home.

Wonderful?

Nothing about Allegra was wonderful to her father. Nothing. What was wonderful to him now was his young wife Elena—only two years older than Allegra—and their new baby Nico, who apparently weren't expected back from Athens until later that evening as Elena was visiting her parents. And since little Nico's christening wasn't until tomorrow…

Who was the third glass for?

Allegra slipped her tote bag off her shoulder and let it drop to the leather sofa next to her, the fine hairs on the back of her neck standing up. 'What's going on?'

Her father smiled. Admittedly it didn't go all the way to his eyes, but then the smiles he turned her way rarely did. He had a habit of grimacing instead of smiling at her. As though he was suffering some sort of gastric upset. 'Can't a father be pleased to see his own flesh and blood?'

When had he ever been pleased to see her? And when had she ever felt like a valued member of the family? But she didn't want to stir up old hurts. Not this weekend. She was home for the christening and then she would fly back to her life in London first thing Monday morning. A weekend was all she was staying. She found it too suffocating, staying any longer than that, and even that was a stretch. She glanced at the champagne flutes on the tray. 'So who's the third glass for? Is someone joining us?'

Her father's expression never faltered but Allegra couldn't help feeling he was uneasy about something. His manner was odd. It wasn't just his overly effusive greeting but the way he kept checking his watch and fidgeting with the cuff of his sleeve, as if it was too tight against his wrist. 'As a matter of fact, yes. He'll be here any moment.'

Something inside Allegra's heart kicked against her chest wall like a small cloven hoof. 'He?'

Her father's mouth lost its smile and a frown brought his heavy salt-and-pepper eyebrows into an intimidating bridge. 'I hope you're not going to be difficult. Draco Papandreou is—'

'*Draco* is coming here?' Allegra's heart kicked again but this time the hoof was wearing steel caps. 'But why?'

'Elena and I have asked him to be Nico's godfather.'

Allegra double blinked. She had thought it a huge compliment when her father and his wife had asked her to be their little son's godmother. She'd assumed it was Elena's idea, not her father's. But she hadn't realised Draco was to be Nico's godfather. She'd thought one of her father's older friends would have been granted the honour. She hadn't realised he considered Draco a close friend these days, only a business associate—or rival, which seemed more appropriate. The Papandreou and Kallas names represented two powerful corporations that had once been close associates, but over the years the increasingly competitive market had caused some fault lines in the relationship.

But Allegra had her own issues with Draco. Issues that meant any meeting with him would be fraught with amusement on his part and mortification on hers. Every time she saw him she was reminded of her clumsy attempt as a gauche teenager to attract his attention by flirting with and simpering over him and, even more embarrassingly, the humiliating way in which he had put a stop to it. 'Why on earth did you ask *him*?'

Her father released a rough-sounding sigh and reached for the shot of ouzo he'd poured earlier. He tipped his head back, swallowed the drink and then placed the glass down with an ominous thud. 'The business is in a bad way. The economic crisis in Greece has hit me hard. Harder than I expected—much harder.

I stand to lose everything if I don't accept a generous bailout merger from him.'

'Draco Papandreou is…is *helping* you?' Every time Allegra said his name a sensation scuttled down her spine like a small sticky-footed creature. She hadn't seen Draco since she'd run into him at a popular London nightspot six months ago where she'd been meeting a date—a date who had stood her up. A fact Draco had showed great mirth in witnessing. *Grr.*

She loathed the man for being so…so *right* about everything. It seemed every time she made one of her stupid mistakes he was there to witness it. After that embarrassing flirtation on her part when she'd been sixteen, she had quickly transferred her attention to another young man in her circle. Draco had warned her about the boy and what had she done? She'd ignored his warning and got her heart broken. Well, not broken, exactly, but certainly her ego had got knocked around a bit.

Then, when she'd been eighteen, Draco had found her helping herself to the notoriously potent punch at one of her father's business parties she was supposed to have been helping him host and had lectured her about drinking too much. Another lecture she'd wilfully ignored…and, yes, he'd been there to see her coughing up her lungs a short time later. Double *grr.* Admittedly, he'd been rather handy with a cool face cloth and had gently held her hair back from her face…

But it hadn't stopped her hating him.

Not one little bit.

Even in all the years since, when she ran into him he had an annoying habit of treating her as if she was still that gauche teenager and not a grown woman with a high-flying legal career in London.

'Draco has offered me a deal,' her father said. 'A business merger that will solve all my financial problems.'

Allegra gave a disdainful snort. 'It sounds too good to be true, which usually means it is. What does *he* want out of it?'

Her father didn't meet her gaze and turned slightly to pour another drink instead. She knew her dad well enough to know he only drank to excess in one of two states: relaxed or stressed. Stressed seemed to be the ticket this time. 'He has some conditions attached,' he said. 'But I have no choice but to accept. I have to think of my new family—Nico and Elena don't deserve to be punished for my misfortune. I've done all I can to hold off the creditors, but it's at crisis point. Draco is my only lifeline...or at least the only one I'm prepared to take.'

His new family. Those words hurt her more than she wanted to admit. When had she ever felt part of his *old* family? She'd been a 'spare part' child. A rescue plan, not a person. Her older brother Dion had contracted leukaemia as a toddler, and back in those days parents had been encouraged to have another child in case the new baby was a bone-marrow match. Needless to say, Allegra hadn't come up with the goods. She had failed on both counts. Not a match. Not male. Dion had died before Allegra was two years old. She didn't even remember him. All she remembered was she had been brought up by a series of nannies because her mother had been stricken with unrelenting grief. A grief that had morphed into depression so crippling, Allegra had been sent to boarding school to 'give her mother a break'.

Her mother had 'accidentally' taken an overdose of sleeping tablets the day before Allegra was to have come home for the summer the year she turned twelve. No one had said the word 'suicide' but she had always believed her mother had intended to end her life that day. The hardest part for Allegra was the sad realisation she hadn't been enough for her mother. Her father hadn't even bothered to hide his disappointment in having a female heir instead of the son he had worshipped. Hardly a day had gone by during her childhood and adolescence when Allegra hadn't felt the sting of that disappointment.

But now her father had moved on with a new wife and a new baby.

Allegra had never belonged and now even less so.

'Draco will tell you about our agreement himself,' her father said. 'Ah, here he is now.'

Allegra whipped around to see Draco's tall figure enter the room. Her eyes met his onyx gaze and a strange sensation spurted and then pooled deep and low in her belly. Every time she looked at him she had exactly the same reaction. Her senses jumped to attention. Her pulse raced. Her heart flip-flopped. Her breath hitched as though it were attached to strings and someone was jerking them. Hard.

He was wearing casual clothes: sandstone-coloured chinos and a white shirt rolled past his strong, tanned forearms, which took nothing away from his aura of commanding authority. When Draco Papandreou walked into a room every head turned. Every female heart fluttered…as hers was doing right now, as though there were manic moths trapped in her heart valves. He oozed sex appeal from every cell of his six-foot-

three frame. She could feel it calling out to her feminine hormones like an alpha wolf calling a mate. No
other man had ever made her more aware of her body
than him. Her body seemed to have a mind of its own
when he came anywhere near.

A wicked mind.

A mind that conjured up images of him naked and
his long, hair-roughened legs entwined with hers. The
only way she could disguise the way he made her feel
was to hide behind a screen of sniping sarcasm. He
thought her a shrew, but so what? Better that than let
him think she was secretly lusting after him. That the
embarrassing crush she had foolishly acted on when
she'd been sixteen had completely and utterly disap-
peared. That her dreams didn't feature him in various
erotic poses doing all sorts of X-rated things with her.
She would rather be hanged and quartered and her
body parts posted to the four corners of the earth than
admit the only sex she'd had in the last year or so had
been by herself, with him as her fantasy.

That—God help her—the last time she'd had sex
with a partner it had been Draco she had thought of
the whole time.

'Draco, how nice of you to gate crash a private family celebration. No hot date tonight with one of your
bottle-blonde bimbos?'

His mouth lifted at one corner in his signature half-
cynical, half-amused smile. 'You're my date, *agape
mou*. Hasn't your father told you?'

Allegra gave him a look that would have snap-
frozen a gas flame. 'Dream on, Papandreou.'

His dark eyes glinted as if the thought of her saying
no to him secretly turned him on. That was the trouble

with having had a crush on a man since you'd been a pimple-spotted teenager. They *never* let you forget it. 'I have a proposal to put to you,' he said. 'Would you like your father present or shall I do it in private?'

'It's immaterial to me where you do it because nothing you propose to me would ever in a thousand, million, squillion years evoke the word "yes" from me,' Allegra said.

'Er… I think I can hear one of the servants calling me,' her father said and left the room with such haste it looked as though he were running from an explosion. But then, whenever she and Draco were left alone together the prospect of an explosion was a very real possibility.

Draco's gaze held hers in a tether that made the base of her spine shiver. 'Alone at last.'

Allegra broke the eye contact, walked over to the drinks tray and casually poured a glass of champagne. Or at least she hoped it looked casual. She wasn't a big drinker but right now she wanted to suck on that bottle of champagne until it was empty. Then she wanted to throw the bottle at the nearest wall. Then the glasses, one by one, until they shattered into thousands of shards. Then every stick of furniture in the room.

Smash. Bash. Crash.

Why was he here? Why was he helping her father? What could it possibly have to do with her? The questions tumbled through her brain like the champagne tumbling into her glass. Her father's business was hanging in the balance? How could that be? It was one of the most well-established businesses in Greece, and had operated for several generations. Other business people looked up to him, in awe of all he had achieved.

Her father had always brandished his wealth like it was a ten-thousand-strong flock of golden-egg-laying geese. How had it come to this?

Allegra turned and gave Draco a sugar-sweet smile. "Can I offer you a drink? Weed killer? Liquid nitrogen? Cyanide?'

He gave a deep rumble of a laugh that did strange things to her insides. Things they had no business doing. Not for him. 'Under the circumstances, champagne would be perfect.'

She poured a glass and handed it to him, annoyed her hand wasn't quite steady. He took the glass but in doing so his fingers brushed against hers. It was like being touched with a live current. The shock of it sent a jolt through her entire body, making her hormones sit up and beg for more. She snatched her hand back and then wished she hadn't. He had an uncanny ability to read her body language like a cryptographer reading code.

Everything about him unsettled her. Made her feel things she didn't want to feel. But no matter how hard she fought it she couldn't take her eyes off him. It was as though magnets were attached to her eyeballs and he was true north. She had seen a lot of beautiful men over the years but no one came close to having Draco's pulse-tripping features. Ink-black hair with just enough curl to make her want to run her fingers through it and straighten out those sexy kinks. A mouth that was not just sensual but sinfully sculpted. A mouth that made her think of long, drugging kisses. The mere thought of his hard male mouth crushing hers was enough to make her get all hot and bothered and breathless.

She had felt that mouth on hers. Once. Had felt it and

had responded to it, only to have him push her away with an ego-crushing comment about how a silly little girl like her could never satisfy a man like him. For years that cruel put-down had savaged her self-esteem. It had ruined her sexual confidence—not that she'd had much to begin with. Damn him for being so darned attractive. Why couldn't she stop gawping at him as if she were still that stupid, star-struck kid with a crush?

He had shaved but the potent male hormones surging around his body would be enough to defeat any decent razorblade. Dark stubble was peppered along his lean jaw and around his mouth.

Dear God, she had to stop looking at his mouth.

She picked up her glass of champagne but before she could take a sip he held his glass within reach of hers. 'To us.'

Allegra pulled her glass back before it could touch his, sloshing the champagne down the front of her blouse. Of course, she was wearing silk. The saturating liquid made her right breast stand out even though it was inside a lace bra. Why was she so ridiculously clumsy around him? It was mortifying. She brushed off the excess liquid with her hand but it only made the dampness worse, making the upper curve of her breast cling to the fabric as though she were in a wet T-shirt competition.

Draco handed her a clean white handkerchief. Of course he would be carrying a clean white handkerchief. 'Would you like me to—?'

Allegra snatched the square of cloth off him before he could finish the sentence. No way was she letting him touch her breast even if it was through four folds of cotton. She couldn't guarantee a suit of armour and

Kevlar vest would keep her from responding to his touch. She dabbed at her wet breast and never had such a task seemed so erotic. Even her breast thought so. It was tingling and her nipple peaking…but maybe that was because Draco's dark obsidian gaze was following her every movement over it. She screwed the handkerchief into a tight ball and tossed it to the coffee table. 'I'll have it laundered and returned to you.'

'Keep it as a souvenir.'

'The only souvenir I want from you is the word "goodbye".'

His eyes held hers again in a spine-shuddering, resolve-melting lock. 'The only way that's going to happen is if I pull out of this business merger.'

'I don't care about the merger.'

'Maybe not, but you should. It rests solely on your compliance with the terms of the deal.'

Terms? What terms?

Allegra disguised her unease by shaking her loose hair back behind her shoulders in a gesture of indifference. But she was far from indifferent. Something about his unwavering gaze made her feel he was toying with her, like a cat with a mouse it had cleverly cornered. What on earth could he want her compliance over?

Since *that kiss* years before, there had always been a climate of tension between them. A tug of war of wills. A power struggle that crackled the air when they were in the same room together. He was her enemy and she didn't care who knew it. Hating him made it easier for her to forget how much she'd wanted him. Hating him kept her safe from her own traitorous hormones that were annoyingly, persistently, immune to every other man but him. 'My father's business affairs are of no concern to me. I am completely independent of him and have been for the last ten or so years.'

'Independent financially, maybe, but you're his only daughter. His only child. He paid for your stellar education. He gave you everything money could buy. Don't you care he's about to lose everything without my help?' His deeply carved frown added to the grave delivery of his words.

Allegra wished she didn't care. But the trouble was, she did. It was her Achilles' heel—her weak spot, the raw, vulnerable part of her personality—the need to feel loved and valued by her only living parent. She had sought it all her life to no avail. In spite of her father's shortcomings, inside she was still that small child looking for his approval. Pathetic, but true. 'I fail to see what any of this has to do with me. I simply don't care what state my father's business is in.' She knew she sounded cold and unfeeling but why should she care what Draco thought of her?

He studied her for a long moment. 'I don't believe you. You do care. Which is why you'll agree to marry me to keep the business afloat.'

Shock hit her in the chest like a punch. *Marry him?* Allegra widened her eyes. Not saucer-wide. Not dinner-dish-wide. Platter-dish-wide. Surely he hadn't just said that? The M word? Him and her? Married? To each other? She blinked and then laughed but even to her ears it sounded on the verge of hysterical. 'If you think for one second I would marry anyone, let alone you, then you are even more of an egomaniac than I thought.'

Draco's gaze continued to hold hers in an intractable

lock that was a tantalising tickle to her girly bits. 'You will do it, Allegra, or see your father's business die a slow and painful death. It's on life support as it is. I've been drip-feeding your father money for the last year. He hasn't got the funds to repay me even if I waive the interest. No one will lend him anything now, not after the way things have panned out in our economy. I came up with this solution instead. This way everyone wins…in particular, you.'

Allegra couldn't believe his arrogance. Did he really think she would agree to such a preposterous deal? She hated him with a passion. She couldn't think of a single person she would *less* like to marry. Well, she could, given her line of work, but that wasn't the point. He was a playboy. A fast-living Lothario who churned through women like a speed-reader churned through cheap paperbacks. Marriage to Draco would be emotional suicide, even if she didn't hate him. 'You're unbelievable. What planet are you on that you would think I would see this as a win for me? Marriage isn't a win for any woman. It's a one-way ticket to serfdom, that's what it is, and I won't have a bar of it.'

'You've been hanging around divorce courts way too long,' he said. 'Plenty of marriages work well for both parties. It could work for us. We have a lot in common.'

'The only thing we have in common is we both breathe oxygen,' Allegra said. 'I dislike everything about you. Even if I were on the hunt for a husband, I would never consider someone like you. You're the sort of man who would expect his pipe and slippers brought to him when he gets home. You don't want a wife, you want a servant.'

His half-smile was back, making his impossibly black eyes twinkle. 'I love you too, *glykia mou*.'

Allegra thinned her gaze to hairpin slits. 'Read my lips. I am not marrying you. Not to save my father's business. Not for any reason. No. No. No. No.'

Draco took a leisurely sip of his champagne and put the glass down on the coffee table with exacting precision. 'Of course, you'll have to commute between London and my home for work, but you can use my private jet—that is, if I'm not using it myself.'

Allegra clenched her hands into fists. 'Are you listening to me? I said I am *not* marrying you.'

He sat on the sofa and leaned back with his hands behind his head, one ankle crossed over the other with indolent grace. 'You haven't got a choice. If you don't marry me then your father will blame you for the collapse of his company. It's a good company but it's been badly run of late. That business manager your father appointed a couple of years ago when he had that health scare didn't do him any favours. I can undo that damage and turn the business around so it's profitable again. Your father will stay on the board and have a share of the profits I guarantee will be more than he has received in decades.'

Allegra bit down on her lip. It had been a worrying time when her father had had a cancer scare. She had flown back and forth as much as she could to help him through his bout of chemo and radiation. Not that he'd shown any great appreciation, of course. But to marry Draco to save her father from financial ruin? It was as if she had suddenly stepped into the pages of a Regency novel.

But her father needed her. *Really* needed her. There

could have been worse men than Draco to offer for her, she had to admit. The sort of men she faced down in court. Mean men. Dangerous men. Men who had no respect for women and who used their children as weapons and pay-backs. Men who stalked, bullied, threatened and even killed to get their own way.

Draco might be arrogant but he wasn't mean. Dangerous? Well, maybe to her senses, yes. Her senses went into a dazzled and dizzying frenzy when he came close. Which was a very good reason why she couldn't marry him.

Wouldn't marry him.

'Why me?' Allegra said. 'Why would you possibly want me for a wife when you can have any woman you want?'

His eyes did a lazy sweep of her from head to foot and back again, sending a frisson through every cell in her body. 'I want you.'

Those sexily drawled words should not have made her feminine core do a happy dance. She wasn't vain but knew she was considered attractive in a classical sort of way. She had her mother's English peaches-and-cream complexion, her dark blue eyes and slim build, but she had her father's jet-black hair and drive to achieve.

But Draco dated super-models, starlets and nubile nymphets. Why would he want to shackle himself to a hard-nosed career woman like her, especially when they fought at every chance they got?

Over the years she had done her level best to hide her attraction to him. The Embarrassing Incident when she'd been sixteen was filed away in her mind in the drawer marked 'Do Not Open'. These days she sneered instead of simpered. She derided instead of drooled. She flayed instead of flirted.

Falling in love with Draco Papandreou would be asking for the sort of trouble she helped other women extricate themselves from on a daily basis. Love did weird things to women. They got blindsided, hood-winked, charmed into looking at their men through rosy love-tinted glasses that failed to show up their faults until it was too late.

Allegra wasn't going to be one of those women—a victim of some man's power game, leaving her as vulnerable as a rain-soaked kitten. 'Listen, I appreciate the compliment, such as it is, but I'm not in the marriage market. Now, if you'll excuse me, I'm going to—'

'The offer is for today and today only. After that I start asking for my money back. With interest.'

She sent her tongue over her lips but they felt as dry as the cardboard cover on one of her expert reports. The economic crisis in Greece was serious. So serious that many well-established companies had hit the wall like over-ripe peaches. She might have some issues with her father but not to the point where she wanted to see him ruined and publicly humiliated. Not now he had a wife and young baby to provide for. Allegra liked Elena. She hadn't expected to, with Elena only being two years older than her, but she did. It some ways Elena reminded her of herself—trying too hard to please everyone in an effort to be loved and accepted.

But if she married Draco to save her father from financial destruction she would be exposing herself to the sort of sensual danger she could well do without. For years she'd kept her distance from him. After that mortifying encounter when she was sixteen, it was her only way of protecting herself. But how would she keep her distance if she were married to him? 'This marriage you're…erm…proposing…' It was lowering to find her voice sounding so scratchy. 'What do you get out of it?'

His eyes shone with a devilish gleam that made her inner thighs tingle as if he had stroked her intimately. No one else could do that to her. Turn her on with a look. Make her so hungry for him she had trouble keeping her hands off him. She would like nothing more than to run her hands all over that strong male body to see if it was as deliciously hard and virile as it looked. When had she not burned with lust for him? Ever since she'd been a teenager with newly awakened hormones he'd been her go-to fantasy guy. No one else came close. He had all but ruined her for anyone else and he hadn't so much as touched her, other than incidentally, since that kiss. 'I get a wife who's hot for me. What more could a man want?'

Allegra kept her expression under tight control. 'If you want a trophy wife then why not select one from your crowd of sexy little sycophants?'

'I want a wife with a brain between her ears.'

'Any woman with half a brain would steer clear of a man like you.'

Her insult only made his smile tilt further, as if he was enjoying himself at her expense. 'And if you were to provide me with an heir…'

'A…what?' Allegra's voice came out like a mouse's squeak. 'You're expecting me to have…?'

'Now that I think about it…' He rose from the sofa with leonine agility. 'An heir and a spare might be a good thing, *ne*?'

Was he teasing or was he serious? It was so hard to

tell behind the sardonic screen of his gaze. 'Aren't you forgetting something? I don't want children. I have a career I'm not prepared to sacrifice for a family.'

'Lots of women say that but in most cases it's not true. They say it as an insurance policy in case no one asks them to marry them.'

Allegra's mouth dropped open so far, she thought her toenails would be bruised. 'Are you for real? What jungle vine did you just swing down from? Women are not breeding machines. Nor are we waiting around with bated breath for some man to stick a ring on our finger and carry us off to be their domestic slave. We have just as much ambition and drive as men, some-times even more so.'

'I'm all for your drive.' His eyes did that glinting thing again. 'That's another thing we have in common, *ne*?'

The less she thought about his sex drive, the better. No one oozed it more potently than him. He was the poster boy for pick-up sex. He moved from relationship to relationship faster than a driver late for an important appointment changed lanes. What had brought about this sudden desire to play family man? He was only thirty-four—three years older than her. Or was it his way of twisting her arm? The arm that was attached to her hormone-charged body that strangely—since that night six months ago in London—kept reminding her every time she had a period she was over thirty and childless. 'I don't know where you got the idea I would agree to this farcical plan. Did my father suggest it?'

'No, it was entirely my idea.'

His idea? Allegra frowned. 'But you don't even like me.'

He came and stood in front of her, his superior height making her feel like a child's rocking horse standing up to a Clydesdale stallion. He didn't touch her but she could feel the magnetic pull of his body making every cell in hers gravitate towards him. She raised her eyes to his, momentarily losing herself in those bottomless pools of black with their fringe of thick lashes.

Why did he have to be so wickedly attractive? Why did her hormones jump up and down in ecstatic glee when he was close? Her gaze went to his mouth, drinking in the way his lips were both firm yet sensually supple, the lower one generous, the top one slimmer, but not enough to be considered cruel. It was a mouth always on the verge of a smile, as if he found life amusing rather than sad. Had she ever seen a more kissable male mouth?

'We could be good together, *agape mou*. Very good.'

Allegra suppressed the shiver his provocative words evoked. His voice was deep and mellifluous and his Greek accent—so much stronger than the faint trace of it in her voice—never failed to make her skin prickle in delight.

He always spoke English to her because she had let her Greek slip after living so long in England. She understood it more than she could speak it but she could hardly describe herself as fluent. She had always spoken English to her Yorkshire-born mother and she suspected her neglect of her father's language was a subconscious way to punish him for not being the father she longed for. 'Look, Draco, this has to stop. All this talk of a marriage between us is pointless. I'm not—'

He took one of her hands and enfolded it in the cage of his. His fingers were warm and dry, the tensile strength in them making something in her stomach drop like a book falling from a shelf. Make that a dozen legal textbooks. Who knew her hand was so sensitive? It was as if every nerve was on the outside of her skin, tingling, making her aware of every pore of his. 'Why are you so frightened of getting close to me?'

Allegra had to swallow a couple of times to find her voice. 'I—I'm not frightened of you.' *I'm frightened of me. Of how you make me feel.*

His thumb began a slow stroke of the fleshy base of hers. It was as light as a sable brush on a priceless canvas but it triggered an explosion of sensations that ricocheted through her body. Her heart picked up its pace as though she'd been given a shot of adrenalin with a crack chaser. Her brain was scrambled by his closeness, her resolve to keep her distance gone missing without leave.

His eyes searched hers for a long, pulsing moment. It was as if he was committing every one of her features to memory: the shape of her eyes, her nose, her cheeks, her mouth and the tiny beauty spot just above the right side of her top lip.

Allegra licked her lips, then realised what a blatant giveaway that was—the primary signal of attraction. It was as if her body was acting of its own accord. Her will, her determination to resist him, was overridden by a primal need to touch him, to have him touch her. To have him kiss her until she forgot about everything but how those firm, male lips felt on hers.

What are you doing?

The alarm bell of her conscience shattered the moment and she pushed against his chest and stepped back to create some distance between them. 'Don't even think about it, buddy.'

His mouth tilted in a knowing smile. 'I'm a patient man. The longer I wait, the better the satisfaction.'

Allegra had a feeling there would be a heck of a lot of satisfaction going on if she were to submit to his passion. The sort of satisfaction that had mostly eluded her in her previous encounters. She wasn't good at sex, or at least not with a partner. She could get things working fairly well on her own, but with a partner she found it too distracting to orgasm. Dead embarrassing, but at least she had been able to fudge her way through it. So far.

But she suspected Draco wouldn't be fooled.

Not for a minute.

Allegra refilled her glass for something to do with her hands. She was conscious of him watching her every move, his dark gaze resting on her like a caress. Her skin tingled, her pulse raced, her insides coiled tight with need. A need awakened by him. 'I think it's best if we forget we had this conversation. I don't want anything to spoil Nico's christening tomorrow.'

'What will spoil it will be you refusing to marry me to save your father's skin,' Draco said. 'You haven't got a choice, Allegra. He needs you like he's never needed you before.'

It was far more tempting than she wanted to admit. Not just because of how it would make her father finally appreciate her, but because she couldn't stop thinking about what it would be like to be Draco's wife. Sharing his life with him, sharing his luxury villa on his own private island. Sharing his body. Being pleasured by him, experiencing the full gamut of human passion. It was a dream come true for the gauche teenager she had once been.

However, she wasn't that girl any more.

But then a thought dropped into her head. Had her father and Elena only asked her to be godmother to Nico because of Draco and his offer? Would they have asked her without the merger and the marriage condition? Wasn't she good enough on her own to be Nico's godmother? Why did she have to partner with her enemy? A man she loathed with the same passion she desired him.

Allegra twirled her glass and placed it back down on the tray next to the champagne bottle. 'Here's a hypothetical question for you. If I were to marry you then how long would you expect the marriage to last?'

'For as long as I want it to.'

And how long would that be? Allegra turned to look at the view from the window to give herself more time to think. The sunlight was so bright it was almost violent. The intense blue of the Aegean Sea, and the equally vivid blue domes in contrast to the stark white of the houses, never failed to snatch her breath. It was picture-postcard perfect, especially from her father's luxury villa in Oia, where the best sunsets in the world were occurred.

It was home and yet it wasn't.

She'd always felt like she had a foot in both countries and it added to her sense of not really belonging anywhere.

If she married Draco to save her father from financial disgrace, where would that leave her when it was time to call an end to their marriage? Few marriages ended with a mutual agreement to part. There was nearly always one party who wasn't happy about the break-up. Would that be her? And—if he wasn't joking about the heir he said he wanted—there was no way she would have a child under such circumstances, with the knowledge that the marriage had no guarantee, no promise of full and lasting commitment.

Allegra turned back to look at Draco. 'Still speaking hypothetically here. What about my career? Or do you expect me to give that up?'

'No, of course not,' he said. 'But there will have to be compromises occasionally. I have business interests in London, as you know, but most of my time is spent in Greece. I think the fact you have your own career will enhance our marriage rather than complicate it.'

'And you would expect me to be with you most of the time?' Allegra said it as though it was the most unreasonable request in the world. As though she'd be committing to daily root-canal treatment.

His expression flickered with amusement. 'Isn't that what husbands and wives do?'

Allegra sent him a speaking look. 'Ones that are in love with each other, maybe. But that hardly applies in our case.'

One side of his smile went a little higher. 'You've been in love with me since you were a teenager. Go on—admit it. That's why you haven't got married yet or dated with any regularity. You can't find anyone that does it for you like I do it for you.'

Allegra affected a laugh. '*Seriously?* That's what you think?' What signals had she been giving off to make him think she was still that clumsy teenage girl?

She wasn't that infatuated fool any more. She was all grown up and she hated him. Hated. Hated. Hated him.

His eyes gleamed like wet paint. 'When was the last time you slept with a man?'

She folded her arms across her body and pursed her lips like she was a schoolmistress staring down an impertinent child. 'I'm not going to give you details of my sex life. It's none of your damn business who I sleep with.'

'It will be my business once we're married. I expect you to be faithful.'

Allegra unfolded her arms and planted her hands on her hips instead. 'And what about you? Will you be faithful or will I have to turn a blind eye to your little dalliances like my mother did for my father?'

Something hardened around his mouth, making it appear flatter, less mobile. 'I am not your father, Allegra. I take the institution of marriage very seriously.'

'So seriously you're prepared to marry a woman you don't love, for a short period of time, just so you can acquire a flagging business?' She made a scoffing noise. 'Don't make me laugh. I know why you want to marry me, Draco. You want a trophy wife. A wife who knows which knife and fork to use. A wife you can take anywhere without worrying she might embarrass you. Then, when you've got me to pop out an heir, you'll get bored, send me on my way and keep the kid. I'm not doing it. No way. Find some other puppet.'

She pushed past him to leave the room but he snagged her wrist on her way past, bringing her around to face him. Her skin burned where his fingers gripped her, but not a painful burn, more of a sizzling, tingling burn that sent heat rushing through her body and pooling in her core. He had rarely touched her since that kiss other than by accident. The contact of his flesh on hers was like being zapped with a lightning bolt. It made every nerve beneath her skin pirouette. His thumb found her thrumming pulse and soothed it with slow, measured strokes while his eyes held hers prisoner.

'I was only teasing about the heir,' he told her. 'But think carefully, Allegra. Yes, I am in the market for a suitable wife, and you fit the bill. But this is also your chance to get your father to finally notice you. You won't just be helping him, but Elena and little Nico, by providing them with security. If the business goes under, it will take them down with it.'

He had found another weak spot. Elena and Nico. They were the innocents in this situation and their future would be compromised if she didn't do something. Allegra could offer her father a loan but the sort of money Draco was talking about was in the millions. Many millions. She was wealthy, but not wealthy enough to float a multi-million-euro corporation. She let out a rattling breath and looked down at their joined hands. How could she turn her back on her father's financial plight when she was the only person who could do something? If her father went down, Elena and darling little Nico would be collateral damage. She couldn't stand back and let that happen. Not when she could help it. She would have to marry Draco. *Gulp.* 'It seems I don't have any choice.'

Draco brought her chin up so her gaze meshed with his. 'You won't regret it. I can guarantee it.'

You think? Allegra brushed his hand away from her chin and took a step backwards. 'I'm not agreeing to this for any other reason than to save my family. Are you absolutely clear on that?'

His eyes shone with a triumphant gleam that made the backs of her knees tingle. 'But of course.'

She disguised a swallow, trying not to notice the way his eyes kept glancing at her mouth. 'When are you thinking of…doing it? I mean, getting married?'

'I have already taken the liberty to make all the arrangements. We'll be married next weekend. I would have done it this one but I didn't want to steal little Nico's limelight.'

Allegra's eyes bulged in alarm. 'So soon?'

'It is a little rushed, but it will be a relatively simple affair. Just a handful of close friends and family.'

'But what if I want the whole shebang?'

'Do you?'

She blew out another breath and averted her gaze. 'No…'

'You'd be surprised at what can be done in a short period of time when you have money. If you want a white wedding, then that's what you will have.'

Allegra had never been the sort of girl to hanker after the fairy-tale wedding. She had rarely even thought of getting married. Her career had always been her top priority. She normally avoided bridal shops and didn't drool at jewellers' windows. But ever since she'd been a bridesmaid at a friend's wedding a couple of months ago she had started to think about what it would be like to be a bride. To be loved by someone so much they would promise to spend the rest of their life with her. It was indeed a fairy tale, one she saw turn to ashes and heartache every day of her working life.

'We'll be married on my island retreat,' Draco said. 'It will be easier to keep the press away.'

Allegra had never been to Draco's private retreat but she had seen photos. He had a villa in Oia, an apartment in Athens and other homes on Kefalonia and Mykonos. But his secluded retreat on his private island had the most amazing gardens and an infinity pool that was perched on the edge of a vertiginous cliff. It would make a stunning wedding location.

And a perfect spot for a honeymoon.

Do not even think about the honeymoon.

'Aren't you worried what the press will make of us?' Allegra asked.

He gave a loose-shouldered shrug. 'Not particularly. I've grown accustomed to them speculating on my private life. Most of the time they make stuff up.'

Not everything was fiction. She had seen enough photos of him surrounded by beautiful women to know he wasn't living the life of a Tibetan monk. Far from it. He was considered one of Greece's most eligible bachelors. Women were elbowing each other out of the way to score a date with him. What would everyone say when they heard *she* was to be his wife? A single-minded career woman like her, marrying a fast-living playboy like him.

It was laughable.

'You'll have to take a week off work, of course,' he said. 'We'll take a short honeymoon on my yacht.'

Her heart flapped like a goldfish trapped in the neck of a funnel. 'Hang on a minute—why do we need to have a honeymoon?'

There was a spark of something at the back of his gaze. Something dark and sensual and spine-tinglingly wicked. 'If you need me to spell that out for you, *agape mou*, then you've been living an even more cloistered life than I thought.'

Allegra crossed her arms, holding them tightly against her stomach. *A honeymoon? On his yacht?* His yacht was no cheap little fishing dingy, but it could never be large enough for her to feel safe. Safe from her own wicked, traitorous desires. She would need a cruise liner or an aircraft carrier for that and even that would be no guarantee. 'Look, I'm prepared to marry you for the sake of my father, but I'm not going to sleep with you. It will be an on-paper marriage. A marriage in name only.'

Draco came back to where she was standing but she had moved back against the wall, which gave her nowhere to escape. And with her hands crossed over her body she didn't have room to unwind them to push him away. She breathed in the scent of him—lime and cedar with a hint of something that was unique to him. It unfurled around her nostrils, making them flare to take more of him in. She felt drunk on him. Dazzled by the pheromones that swirled and heated and mated with hers.

He slipped a hand to the side of her head, his fingers splaying through her hair until every root on her scalp shivered in delight. His eyes had that dark, twinkling spark of amusement that did so much damage to her resolve. Lethal damage. Irreparable damage. 'And how long do you think an on-paper marriage between us would last, hmm?' His voice was a deep burr that grazed the length of her spine like a caress from one of his work-callused hands. 'I want you and I intend to have you.'

Allegra couldn't stop staring at his mouth—the way his lips shaped around every word; the way his stubble made her want to press her mouth to his skin to feel the sexy rasp of his regrowth. *Kiss me. Kiss me. Kiss me*. The chant was pounding an echo in her blood. She didn't want to be the one to make the first move. Not like she had done all those years ago, when she'd thrown herself at him only to be brutally rejected. She wasn't that girl any more. Making the first move would give him too much power. She could resist him. She could. She could. She could.

As if he could read her mind, he brought a fingertip to her mouth and traced a slow outline of her lips, setting off a round of miniature fireworks under her skin. 'Such a beautiful mouth. But I'm not sure if you're going to kiss me back or bite me.'

She inched up her chin. 'Try it and see.'

His smile was lazy and lopsided and sent her belly into free fall. But then he tapped her lower lip with his index finger and stepped back. 'Maybe some other time.'

CHAPTER TWO

DRACO PICKED UP his champagne glass because, unless he gave his hands something to do, he knew they would be tempted to jump ahead a few spaces. He could wait. Sure he could. Allegra was all for keeping things on paper but he knew she would crack before the ink was dry on their marriage certificate.

He knew she was attracted to him. She'd had a teenage crush on him, which had amused and annoyed him in equal measure back in the day. He'd been a little ruthless in handling her back then, but he hadn't been interested in messing with a teenager, especially so soon after his break-up with the ex he'd thought he was going to marry. Back then, Allegra had been young and starry-eyed, fancying herself in love, and had needed to be put firmly in her place.

But she was a woman now—a beautiful woman in the prime of her life.

And he wanted her.

Ever since London, Draco had realised Allegra was exactly what he was looking for in a wife. And when her father, Cosimo Kallas, had come to him for help, he had seized his opportunity and made his financial support conditional on marrying her. Besides, there were other men who were circling like sharks for the money her father owed them, men who he knew wouldn't hesitate to go after Allegra next. He couldn't stand by and let one of them force her into their bed to settle the debts he could pay without flinching. Who knew what might happen to her? Her father had angered a lot of his business associates. Draco wasn't going to let anything happen to her because her father was a fool.

Allegra was classy. She was well-educated, she was well-spoken and she was half-Greek. And, with her untouchable air, she was jaw-droppingly gorgeous. She could have graced a catwalk or been found starring on an old-world Hollywood movie set. She walked like a dancer, her slim figure moving effortlessly across the floor. Her glossy black hair was straight and hung almost to her waist. When she moved, it moved with her in a silk curtain that held his gaze like a super-powerful magnet. He couldn't stop himself from imagining that silky black skein draped over his chest, her long, slender legs entwined with his.

Draco suppressed a shudder of anticipation. He was hot for her. Seriously hot. So hot he only had to look at her and his blood would thunder. He couldn't seem to keep his eyes off her. When she'd spilled her champagne, the silk of her blouse clinging wetly to the perfect globe of her breast had made his blood shoot south in a torrent. He had rarely touched her in the past. Since that kiss when she was a teenager, he had respectfully kept his distance because he hadn't wanted any boundaries to be crossed. He had made it clear he wasn't interested back then and he hadn't wanted to give her mixed messages.

Now was different.

Their marriage wouldn't be for ever, just long enough to secure the business and get Allegra out of his system. Draco had nothing against long-term marriage, but he couldn't see himself doing the time.

He had teased Allegra with that talk of an heir to suss out her feelings on the issue of children. It wouldn't be fair to lock her into marriage—even a short-term one—if she was desperate to have kids. Thankfully, she wasn't, and it was the last thing he wanted from this marriage. Given his childhood, he wasn't sure he could ever see himself having a family.

When his mother had died from a gangrenous appendix when Draco was six, he and his father had been a team intent on survival in a world that didn't notice, let alone help, the desperately poor. Draco had a clear memory of walking with his fisherman father past the Kallas corporation headquarters one day only a month before his father's death. His dad had looked up at the building with its shining brass sign and expressed how he wanted Draco to aim high, to dream big and bountiful, to make something of himself so he wouldn't have to struggle the way he had done. When his father had been killed in a boating accident four weeks later, Draco had been left to fend for himself.

But his father's words had stayed with him, motivating him, fuelling his drive and determination. He'd clawed his way out of poverty, working several menial jobs while trying to get an education. At nineteen, he'd part-owned a business, and had gone on to own it fully when the partner had retired. He had gone from strength to strength after that, building and expanding each company he acquired. He was a self-made man and he was proud of it.

No one could say he wasn't a prize catch.

Not now.

And who could be a better wife for him than Allegra Kallas—the daughter of the businessman who owned the corporation his father had singled out that day with such aspiration? Acquiring the company would be a symbol of Draco's success. A token of the dreams and hopes his father had had for him and that he had now fulfilled in his father's honour.

Draco watched her sipping her champagne, sitting there on one of the plush leather sofas. Her long legs were crossed, one racehorse-slim ankle moving up and down in a kicking motion—the only clue she was feeling agitated. Her expression had gone back to her signature cool mask of indifference, which was another thing that secretly turned him on. He was amused how she took that schoolmistress tone with him. When she tried to stare him down with those flashing, unusually dark blue eyes, it made him hard as stone. Harder. He could feel the throb of it even now.

He'd wanted to kiss her. Of course he had. What man with even a trace of testosterone wouldn't want to feel that lusciously soft mouth? He'd tasted those sweet, hot lips once and couldn't wait to do it again. But he knew if he moved too soon it could shift the balance of power. He wanted his ring on her finger. He wanted her hungry. He wanted her begging. He wanted her to be honest about her lust for him. For lust after him she did. He should know the signs because he was experiencing them himself. He couldn't take his eyes off her generous and supple mouth. Couldn't stop thinking about that mouth opening over him, drawing on him, sucking him till he blew like the volcano Santorini was famous for.

Draco met her eyes across the space that separated them. She raised a perfectly groomed eyebrow at him, that starchy, English aristocratic, 'I'm too good for the likes of you' spark in her eyes making him want to carry her off fireman-style and show her just how good he could be for her. 'Another drink to celebrate our engagement, *agape mou*?' he said.

Her mouth was puckered like the drawstrings of an old-fashioned purse. 'Don't call me that. You know you don't mean it.'

He pushed away from the window where he had been leaning. 'Here's the thing—we have to act like a happy couple, even if in private you want to play pistols at dawn.'

Her chin came up to a defiant height. 'No one's going to believe it, you know. Not us. We're known to positively loathe each other.' Her cheeks went a shade darker. 'Especially after that night in London in December.'

He smiled at the memory. It wasn't the first time he'd felt that tingle of attraction. More than a tingle. A shockwave that had left him buzzing for hours afterwards. 'Ah, yes. It wasn't one of your best moments, was it? I was only trying to help and what did I get? A glass of red wine poured in my lap. Hardly the behaviour of a grown woman.'

Her jaw looked as though she were biting down on a metal rod. 'You provoked me. And it was either have that wine in your lap or splashed in your face, and your throat cut with the glass.'

He tut-tutted and shook his head at her as if she were a wilfully disobedient child who consistently disappointed him. 'It seems I may have to teach you how to behave. That will be fun: *Wife Behaviour for Beginners.*'

She sprang off the sofa as if something had bitten her on the behind, throwing him a look that would have stripped tarmac off a road. 'You think you're so smart, manipulating me into this farce of a marriage, but I've got news for you. I will not be a doormat. I will not be treated like a child. I will not sleep with you. Do? You? Understand?'

Draco loved it when she got angry with him. She was always so buttoned up, cool and controlled. But with him she showed the depth of passion in her personality others didn't see. She was feisty, a firebrand with a flaying tongue and a whip-quick wit. He enjoyed their verbal sparring. It was a big turn-on for him. Few women stood up to him or challenged him the way she did. He liked that she had spirit. That she wasn't afraid to lock horns with him.

He would much rather she locked those gorgeous lips on his, but all in good time.

'I understand you're a little apprehensive about sex, but I can assure you, I'm excellent at it.'

Twin pools of bright pink flared on her cheeks. 'I am not apprehensive about sex. I have sex—I have it all the time. I just don't care to have it with you.'

How he wanted to make her eat every one of those words and lick them away with that hot little tongue of hers. He wanted that tongue all over his body. *He wanted. He wanted. He wanted.* It pulsed through him like an ache. He'd been too long between relationships. It had been weeks—no, months—since he'd had sex. He'd been too busy, distracted by work and the dire financial situation Cosimo Kallas was in, to bother about hooking up with anyone.

But now he was ready.

He was so ready he could barely keep his hands off those slim hips, from pulling her against him so she could feel how ready. 'You will share my bed even if you don't share my body to begin with. I won't have my household staff snickering behind my back at my inability to consummate my marriage.'

She glared at him so hotly he thought the champagne in his glass was going to boil. 'If you so much as lay one finger on me, I'll scream loud enough for them to hear me in Albania.'

Draco gave an indolent smile. 'I can guarantee you'll scream, *glykia mou*. You certainly won't be the first. Most women in my bed do.'

Her mouth went into a flat line and her hands clenched into tight little white-knuckled balls. Her whole body seem to vibrate like a child's battery-operated toy. 'I'm surprised you want to wait until we're married. Why don't you throw me to the floor and have your way with me now?'

'Tempting, but alas, I'm a civilised man.' He swept a hand behind him where he'd entered the room earlier. 'See? No knuckle marks along the carpet.'

Her caustic look showed just how uncivilised she thought him. She swung away and put herself behind one of the sofas, as if she needed to barricade herself. 'I suppose you're only making me wait to ramp up the torture quotient.'

'The sort of torture I have in mind will be mutually pleasurable.'

She shook her hair back behind her shoulders in a

haughty manner. The silky swing of it always fascinated him. It was like the swish of a curtain. 'I find it hard to understand how you could want to bed a woman who hates you. It seems a little kinky to me.'

'You don't hate me, Allegra. What you hate is how you can't get your way with me. You need a strong man. Someone who will allow you to express that passionate nature you keep under wraps all the time. I'm that man.'

She gave one of her derisory laughs. 'Hello? We've actually had a women's movement during the last century. Didn't you hear about that or were you too busy clubbing mammoths and dragging them back to your cave?'

Draco's groin tightened at her witty come-back. She always gave as good as she got, which was another reason he thought her perfect wife material. He didn't want a doormat. He didn't want someone who didn't have the spirit to spar with him.

He wanted her.

It was as simple as that. Since he'd seen her in London he had lost interest in other women. He had found the dating scene increasingly boring and predictable. But every encounter, every conversation, with Allegra was full of surprises. She stimulated him physically and intellectually.

He reached into his top pocket and handed her the ring box he'd brought with him. 'That reminds me—I have something for you. If it doesn't fit, I'll have it adjusted.'

She took the box and cautiously opened it, as if whatever was in there might leap out and bite. But then she let out a breath and picked up the diamond

solitaire with almost worshipful fingers. 'It's beautiful.' She looked up at him, her blue eyes showing a hint
of uncertainty he found strangely touching. 'It looks
frightfully expensive...'

Draco shrugged. 'It's just a ring. I threw a dart at
the counter. This was the one it hit.'

She slipped the ring over her knuckle. 'It fits.'

'Must be an omen.'

Her gaze flicked to his. 'I'll give it back when we
divorce.'

Draco didn't want her thinking there was any hint
of romance in his choice of a ring. He'd done that once
and it had been the worst mistake of his life. 'Keep it.
I'm not sure any future bride of mine would want to
wear a second-hand ring.'

She opened and closed her mouth, as if she couldn't
find what to say. Then she looked down at the ring
winking on her hand. It was a moment before she looked
up at him again. 'How can I be sure you won't play
around while we're married? You've played around all
your adult life. Men like you get bored with one lover.'

Right now, Draco couldn't imagine ever being bored
by her, but it didn't mean he would propose anything
long-term. Long-term was for the in love, and that
hardly described him in this case. He wasn't going to
go down that path ever again. In lust? Yes. Big time.
'When I get bored, I'll let you know. We can end the
marriage before anyone gets hurt.'

'Perhaps I'll get bored first,' Allegra said. 'Women
have the right to choose their own husband, not have
one thrust upon them. If I wanted to choose one, then
you'd be the last man I'd consider. The very last.'

Draco smiled at the insult and moved across to

the door. 'We'd better let your father know the happy news. But, let me remind you, apart from your father no one—and I mean no one—must know this isn't a love match. I'm not interested in the press attention it would receive otherwise.'

Later, Allegra didn't know how she got through the rest of the evening, with Draco and her father chatting away over dinner like two good mates who'd just nailed a successful business deal. Damn it. *She* was the business deal. How could this be happening? Married to her worst enemy! And it was happening so quickly. Her phone hadn't stopped buzzing with incoming messages because Draco had taken the liberty of announcing their engagement on social media. Every platform of social media. *Grr.* It annoyed her because she'd been left looking like an idiot for not saying anything to her friends and colleagues about her 'secret relationship' with Greece's most eligible bachelor.

But when her secretary and best friend Emily Seymour texted, WTF? Is this a joke? Allegra couldn't quite bring herself to lie to her.

No joke but it's not what you think. Will explain later. Can't talk now.

Emily's text came back.

Can't wait! Knew you had a thing for him since that guy was a no-show. He's so HOT!!!'

She'd followed the word 'hot' with an emoticon of flames burning.

Allegra texted back.

MOC. No sex.

Emily sent an emoticon of a person laughing and holding their sides.

Allegra rolled her eyes and typed back.

I mean it!

She put away her phone before she was subjected to any more teasing. She wasn't sure how Emily had picked up on her attraction to Draco. But then, Emily was a bit of a romantic. What signals had Allegra given off? Or was she protesting *too* much?

'Well, I think I'll leave you two to chat while I head off to bed,' Allegra's father said, rising from the table. He paused by Allegra's chair and placed a hand on her shoulder. 'I know you'll be happy with Draco. He's exactly what you need.'

There were a hundred retorts she wanted to throw back but in the end she stayed silent. Her father gave her shoulder a quick pat, as if he were patting a dog he didn't quite trust, before he left the room and quietly closed the door behind him.

Draco twirled the amber contents of his brandy glass, his gaze steady on hers sparkling with amusement. 'Nice to know I've got the father-in-law's big tick of approval.'

Allegra picked up her wine glass and surveyed him over the top of the rim. 'What a pity you don't have mine. But that doesn't seem to matter to you—I wonder why? Maybe you've engineered this because you're secretly in love with me. Is that it?'

His expression became shuttered and he put down his own glass with a soft little thud. 'I'm not sure I'm capable of romantic love. I'm a little too practical for that. But I care about you, if that's any consolation.'

She gave a laugh. 'People *care* about their pot plants. How nice to know you'll offer me water and fertiliser occasionally.'

His crooked smile came back and sparked a sardonic glint in his gaze. 'Whenever you want fertilising, you just let me know.'

Allegra sent him a gimlet glare even though her ovaries were packing their bags and heading to the exits. And it was not just her ovaries that were getting excited. Her feminine core was contracting with a pulsation of lust that made it difficult to sit still in her chair. She had never really thought about having a baby before now. She was a career girl, not an earth mother. An image popped into her head of her belly swollen with his child. His DNA and hers getting it on and producing a baby with dark eyes and dark hair. She saw another image of him holding that baby, his strong arms cradling the tiny bundle while his eyes met hers in a tender look…

She gave herself a mental shake. 'So, you've never been in love? Apart from with yourself, I mean.'

He gave a soft chuckle and draped one arm along the back of the neighbouring chair. 'I'm not averse to a bit of self-love now and again. How about you?'

Allegra wasn't going to give him an account of her sex life even if these days it was mostly with herself. 'I thought I was in love with my first boyfriend but we both know how that ended.' And it had been Draco's fault. Damn him.

'Did you sleep with him?'

'Yes,' she answered in spite of herself.

'And?'

Allegra gave him a 'wouldn't you like to know?' look. 'You think I'm going to swap bedroom tales with you? It was your fault it was such a dis—' She clamped her mouth shut, furious she'd given away more than she'd intended.

'It was consensual…wasn't it?' There was a note of concern in his tone and he moved forward in his chair with a frown pulling at his brow.

'Yes.'

He was still frowning, his posture tense, on edge. 'What happened to make it such a disaster? Is that the word you were going to say?'

Allegra looked at the rim of her glass rather than meet his probing gaze. 'I wanted to get rid of my V card and he seemed the right one to do it with.' She twisted her mouth. 'Obviously these things are easier for you guys. You seem to have fun no matter what.'

'Biology isn't always fair,' Draco said. 'To women especially.'

There was a little silence.

'You were right about him, though,' Allegra said. 'He was such a loser in the end. He told all his mates what a disappointment I'd been in bed. Needless to say, I was completely and utterly mortified.' Why she was telling him that excruciating detail escaped her. Emily was the only other person she had told, because it was too painful to think about, let alone recount to someone else. And too skin-crawlingly embarrassing.

'Yes, well, I reckon he only said that to take the attention off his own inadequacies,' Draco said. 'He should've made your pleasure a priority. That's the golden rule of decent manhood.'

She was pretty certain none of Draco's lovers had ever complained about his lack of prowess in bed. Just the thought of him pleasuring her with that virile body of his was enough to make her get all excited downstairs. But why was she talking about this stuff with him? If she told him much more, he would realise she was practically a nun.

'Fancy an evening stroll out on the terrace?' he asked after a moment, as if he sensed she was uncomfortable with the subject.

'I miss all this when I'm in London,' Allegra said once they were outside and looking at the dark blue, wrinkled silk of the ocean below with its silver band of moonlight shimmering on the surface. 'But then, when I'm here I miss lots of things about London.'

His shoulder brushed against the skin of her bare arm, his left hand within a couple of millimetres of her right one where it was resting on the railing. 'It's a problem when you love two places. That's why I move between the two, so I get the best out of each of them by commuting between seasons. But, of course, not everyone has the financial flexibility to do that.'

The early summer evening air was scented with the salt spray of the sea and the faint but familiar fragrance of the vigorously blooming bougainvillea hanging in a swathe of crimson over the side of the terrace. The far off braying of a donkey and the clanging of the rigging of the yachts in the marina lower down carried in the light, warm breeze.

Allegra stole a covert glance at Draco. The moon-light put his impossibly handsome features into relief, making him look all the more like he had stepped off a marble plinth in an antiquities museum. The high, intelligent forehead with the prominent jet-black eye-brows, the strong nose and sculpted mouth were etched on her brain like a tattoo. What other man had ever compared to him?

It was a cliché, but tall, dark and handsome—and Greek—was her poison. She was lethally attracted to him. She knew it. He knew it. It swirled in the air when they were alone together like a potent but for-bidden drug. One taste and Allegra knew she would be addicted. Which was why she had to keep her dis-tance, even though every cell in her body was trem-bling with the need for contact. It didn't matter how much she fantasised about Draco in secret. No way could she afford to indulge in a physical relationship with him. He had rejected her once. She wasn't going to let him do it again.

But it would be kind of exciting to kiss him...

He turned and saw her looking at him, and before she could put any distance between them he lifted a finger to her face and tucked a breeze-teased tendril of her hair back behind her ear. His face was mostly in shadow, but she could see the moonlight reflected in his gaze like a glint of quartz in black marble.

Allegra knew she should step away, knew too she should brush his hand aside, frown at him and tell him to back off in her sharp, schoolmistress-y tone. But it seemed her mind and body had other ideas. Wicked ideas. Dangerous ideas. Ideas that made her picture her body crushed beneath his, his mouth clamped to hers, their bodies writhing in mutual, skin-shivering ecstasy. She drew closer to him as if someone had a hand in the small of her back, her hips brushing against his. The shock of the erotic contact made her insides twist and coil with lust, her breath hitch and her heart race. She saw her hands slide up to lie flat on his chest, the hard muscles flinching as if her touch electrified him.

Draco's hands went to her waist, his fingers gentle but as hot as a brand. His muscle-dense thighs were so close she could feel their heat and sense their latent strength. His head came down but his mouth hovered rather than landed, his warm, brandy-scented breath mingling with hers.

Allegra sent her tongue out over her lips to moisten them, her whole body poised in that infinitesimal moment before final touchdown.

Go on. Do it. Kiss me and prove that you want me as much as I want you. 'Are you going to kiss me?'

'Thinking about it.' His voice was two parts gravel, one part honey, making her insides quiver.

'What's to think about?' She moved even closer, her breasts, bumping against his chest, making her flesh tingle. 'You know you want to.'

If she was wrong, this was going to be mortifying.

Draco's breath moved in a sexy waft along the side of her mouth, the rasp of his stubble grazing her cheek like fine-grade sandpaper. 'You've had way too much to drink,' he said.

'I'm not drunk—not even tipsy.' *Not on alcohol, that is.*

His tongue glided over her beauty spot, then circled it as if he were circling one of her nipples. A savage jab of lust assailed her, pooling in a liquid heat between her thighs. Then he moved his mouth to her jawbone, his lips working their way up in nibbles and nudge-like movements to the sensitive space below her ear. Her whole body shivered when Draco's teeth gently caught her earlobe, the tender tug sending a riot of sensations in a quick-silver streak down to the base of her spine. Her legs were without bones, without ligaments, trembling to stay upright and only doing so because his hands on her waist were keeping her there.

His mouth kept up its disarming of her senses, taking her on a journey of heady arousal unlike anything she had experienced before. Who knew her jawbone was an erogenous zone? Her jawbone! His lips nibbled their way down to the space between her lower lip and her chin. He was so close to her lips. *So* close… Close enough for them to buzz, tingle and ache for him to cover them with his mouth. But, still, he kept his lips away from hers as if he had made a private vow of kissing celibacy.

Draco's hands moved from her waist to cradle both sides of her head, his fingers splaying under the weight of her hair in a sensual glide that made something at the base of her spine heat, sizzle and melt. 'You are so damn beautiful,' he said in that same deep, gravelly burr.

'So kiss me, then.' Allegra slid her hands around his neck, which brought her lower body flush against his. She could feel the battle going on in his body where it was touching hers—the urge of the primal in combat with his iron will and steely self-control. Her own self-control was nowhere to be seen and she couldn't be bothered to send out a search party.

She wanted him to kiss her.

She needed him to kiss her.

She would *make* him kiss her.

She needed it like she needed her next breath. She would die if Draco didn't give in to the desire she could feel throbbing in his flesh where it was pressed against her. Mutual desire. Dark, wicked desire that refused to go back into its cage now it was released from its prison of denial. If he kissed her it would prove she wasn't the only one who was vulnerable. It would prove he had his weak spot—*her*. This time he wouldn't push her away with a cutting comment. This time she would kiss him as a woman kissed a man, not as a fumbling teenager. She would show him he wasn't as immune to her as he wanted her to think. 'Kiss me, Draco. What are you scared of?'

His hands came back down to settle against her hips, his fingers harder now—possessive, almost. His eyes were sexily hooded, his gaze honed in on her mouth. 'Are you sure you know what you're doing?'

Allegra moved like a sinuous cat against the hard frame of his body, her arms winding around Draco's neck, her fingers tugging, stretching and releasing his black curls. His erection was hot and heavy against her belly, the pounding of his blood echoing the deep, urgent thrumming of her own. She could feel her own moisture gathering, her body preparing itself for the pleasure it craved. Never had she felt desire like it. It was a raging fever, a torrent of need that refused to be ignored. Allegra wasn't going to sleep with him, but one kiss would be enough to take the edge off it, surely? What harm would one kiss do?

'You want me so bad,' she said.

His body pressed harder against her as if he hadn't

the strength of will power to do otherwise. His hands tightened their grip on her hips, his fingers digging into her flesh as if he never wanted to release her. 'Yes. I want you.'

Draco didn't say it out loud, but she could hear the word 'but' somewhere in that statement. Allegra brought her hand around to trace the outline of his mouth, her stomach pitching when the soft pad of her fingertip caught on his stubble. 'I bet you've kissed a lot of women in your time.'

'A few.'

She sent her fingertip down the shallow stubble-covered dip between his lower lip and his chin. Her eyes came back to his intensely dark gaze. 'Did you know you were my first kiss?'

'Not until you kissed me.'

Did he have to remind her how inexpert she had been?

'I've learnt since then. Don't you want to see how much I've improved?'

Allegra sensed he was wavering. He kept silent but his body spoke for him, his desire for her pulsing invisibly in the air like sound waves. His breath mingled with hers. His body was hot and urgent against hers, increasing her hunger for skin-on-skin contact. She slipped her arms back around his neck and rose on tiptoe, bringing her mouth to his in a soft touchdown. When she lifted off, his lips clung to hers like a rough surface to satin. Allegra touched down again, moving her lips against the warm, firm heat of his in an experimental fashion, discovering their texture, their shape. Their danger.

Draco drew in a breath and took control of the kiss,

crushing her lips beneath the fervent pressure of his. His hands went from bracketing her hips to cradling her head, angling it so he could deepen the kiss with a spine-wobbling glide of his tongue through her already parted lips. She welcomed him with a breathless sigh, his tongue tangling with hers in an erotic duel that had unmistakably sexual overtones. Her inner core recognised them, contracting in a fireball of lust that threatened to overwhelm her. Allegra kissed him back with feverish intensity, as if his mouth was her only succour and without it she would cease to exist.

He made a low, growling sound in the back of his throat and explored every inch of her mouth, his tongue sweeping, swirling, diving, darting until her senses were spinning like a top set off by a slingshot. Need ricocheted through her, clamouring to be assuaged. Begging, pleading, to be satisfied with every breath she snatched in while his mouth worked its fiery magic on hers.

One of Draco's hands went to her breast, cupping it in a possessive hold that sent another wave of sensation coursing through her body like sheet lightning. His thumb found her nipple, rolling over it through the fabric of her dress and bra, but she might as well have been naked. The thrill of his touch, even through two layers of fabric, was enough to make Allegra whimper for more. He moved to her other breast, cupping and caressing her through her clothes as if they were star-crossed teenage lovers on a clandestine date. His mouth left hers to blaze a blistering trail of fire down her neck and décolletage, his stubble ticking and tantalising her, his lips and tongue ramping up her desire until she felt like a pressure cooker about to blow.

But, while her self-control was shot to pieces, it seemed his was not.

Draco slowly drew back from her, still holding her in the circle of his arms but without chest-to-chest contact. She felt the loss keenly—her breasts were still tingling from his touch, from being crushed so tightly against his body. She searched his face for a moment but his expression was largely unreadable…all except for that glint of triumph lurking in the depths of his gaze.

Allegra slipped out of his hold and straightened the front of her dress. Time to rein things in. She couldn't allow him to think she was his for the asking. She had proved her point…sort of. But she had a disquieting feeling Draco had proved his own. 'Just to remind you. Kissing is fine, but that's as far as it goes.'

One side of his mouth came up in a slanted smile. 'You seriously think you can maintain that, even if by some remote possibility I agreed to it?'

Allegra raised her chin. 'Those are my rules.'

'Here's what I think of your rules.' He stepped back into her body space, standing close enough for her to feel the tug of attraction pulling at every one of her organs like invisible silken cords. His eyes moved back and forth between both of hers, searching, penetrating, challenging. She drew in a breath but it caught on something in her throat. Her thighs were less than a couple of centimetres from his, her breasts getting all excited about his chest being even closer.

Draco sent a fingertip idly down the slope of her cheek, then continued his tantalising pathway to the fullness of her bottom lip, his finger moving over its already sensitised surface like a mine sweeper. It took all her self-control and more not to take his finger into her mouth, to swirl her tongue around it and draw on it with her lips. The urge to do so was so primal and raw it made her insides quake with need. Allegra licked her lip instead, but her tongue came into contact with his finger on its return journey and an explosion of lust barrelled through her. She gripped the front of Draco's shirt, pressing her body against his, her mouth going to the exposed, tanned skin of his neck, sucking, nibbling, grazing him with her teeth and finally—*dear God, finally*—finding his mouth.

His lips moved with thrilling expertise on hers, his tongue delving deeply to call hers into sensual play. She made little breathless sounds of approval when his hands clasped her by the hips to hold her against his heat. She wanted more. Needed more. She sent her hands on a journey of discovery, sliding them over his hardened length, shaping him through his trousers, her own feminine muscles a frenzy of excitement.

After a moment, Draco placed a hand over hers to stop her from going any further. 'If we play by the rules, then those rules have to be fair.'

Allegra gave a shrug and stepped back, as if she didn't care either way, even though her body was crying out for release and her fingers were aching to feel the weight and heft of him. 'Can't take a little fooling around, Draco?'

His eyes glittered in the darkness. 'I would have you here and now but your father's household staff might be shocked. Don't look now, but his housekeeper Sophia's been watching from the window behind you.'

Allegra's cheeks grew so hot she was sure she was contributing to global warming. How had she let herself behave in such an abandoned way? She prided herself on always acting with poise and decorum around the staff. She wasn't the sort of person to behave recklessly or immodestly. But in Draco's arms she became a wanton woman with no thought for anything other than her body's needs. Needs that still thrummed and hummed inside her like a plucked violin string.

'Well, we are supposed to be acting like a couple in love,' she said. 'I might say you were doing a mighty fine job of it too.'

He gave a soft laugh. 'Don't confuse good old-fashioned lust with love.'

Allegra turned back to look at the ocean cast in its silver glow from the moonlight. She was conscious of Draco standing beside her, close enough for their arms to be touching. Even though his was covered in finely woven cotton, she could still feel the sensual energy of him. The potent vibrancy of him. Couldn't stop imagining how it would feel to have those strong, tanned arms wrapped around her in the grip of passion. 'What if you fall in love with me?' The question was out before she could block it. Had she sounded as if she *wanted* him to fall in love with her?

He turned and leaned his back against the balustrade, his hands resting on the railing either side of his hips. 'We've covered this, Allegra. I'm not sure I'm capable of loving you.'

Allegra flashed him a look. 'How charming of you to say.'

He gave a shrug, as if he recognised the veiled insult but was not going to apologise for it. 'Just saying.'

Of course, Draco falling in love was only a remote possibility. His heart was untouchable. He wasn't the type of man to allow himself to be vulnerable. He was the one who controlled his relationships to a set timetable. Few relationships of his had ever lasted more than a few weeks—one or two, perhaps, a couple of months.

Allegra looked down at her right hand resting next to his on the railing. His skin was so dark and hair-roughened compared to her pale, smoother hand. It was an erotic reminder of all the essential male and female differences between them. If she moved her pinkie a couple of millimetres she would touch him. The temptation to do so was a force inside her body over which she seemed to have little or no control. It was as though he were an industrial-strength magnet and she was a tiny iron filing. He had beautiful hands—broad and dusted with black hair that also lightly touched the backs of his long, strong fingers.

She couldn't stop thinking about those clever hands on her body. Not through her clothes, but on her naked skin. Draco wasn't averse to physical labour. He didn't sit behind a desk all day. He was the sort of man who didn't mind getting his hands dirty at the coalface of the businesses he ran. What would it feel like to have those hands gliding over her flesh? Touching her in places that hadn't been touched in so long she had almost forgotten what it felt like to be a woman?

She sent him a sideways glance. 'Why haven't you been in a long-term relationship before?'

'I have.'

'A month or two is not considered long-term.'

A beat or two of silence passed.

'I had a partner for close to a year once.'

He had? 'Really? I never knew. Gosh, you kept that awfully quiet. The press always—' Allegra thought it best to stop speaking before she revealed how closely she had been following his love-life in the media. It had been a bit of an obsession over the years One she wasn't too proud of, but she'd always had an unhealthy fascination with whomever he was squiring around town and for how long.

There was another long moment of silence.

'I was thinking about asking her to marry me.'

Allegra turned so she was facing him. Draco's face was backlit by the moonlight, so it was hard to make out his expression, but she could see his mouth had a rueful twist to it. 'You were?'

'I even bought the ring.'

She'd never heard even a whisper of an engagement. Why hadn't it been made public? Who wouldn't be interested in a self-made playboy like him settling down? Draco had dragged himself up from abject poverty to become one of Greece's most eligible bachelors. Who was the woman? Who had captured his attention to the degree he would offer to marry her? And, more to the point, why hadn't he gone ahead with the marriage? 'What happened?'

He pushed away from the railing and turned back to look at the moonlit view. She could only see one side of his face but it was enough to make her suspect he didn't like talking about the memory. His features had a boxed-up look about them, the line of his jaw tense, his gaze looking into the far-off distance. 'It turned out she wasn't the one after all.'

'She said no?'

He glanced at his watch and frowned. 'I'd better be on the move. I have some work to do back at my villa before I call it a day.'

Allegra placed her hand on his forearm when he turned from the railing. His muscular arm was warm and the dark, masculine hair faintly prickly under the softer skin of her hand. 'Wait. Tell me what happened.'

Draco went to brush her hand away as if it were a fly but she dug her fingers in. 'Leave it, Allegra.'

No darn way was she going to leave it. Not while she had a chance to find out who he was behind the persona of suave and ruthless businessman. 'I told you about my first time. It wasn't easy talking to you about that, let me tell you. I've only ever told my best friend, Emily. Surely you owe me this one confession?'

It was a moment before he spoke. He stood there looking down at her with her hand on his arm without seeming to move a muscle. But then his arm flexed under her touch and he let out a stream of air that sounded resigned. 'She had someone else lined up. Someone far richer than me. I ended up buying the guy's company a couple of years ago when it got into trouble. Sold it for a profit too. A handsome profit.'

As you do when you're filthy rich and want revenge.

It was a timely reminder to Allegra that the field they were playing on was tipped in his favour. He could be calculating and ruthless when he needed to be. Hadn't Draco already proved that with his non-existent marriage proposal? 'What did your ex think about that?'

He gave a breath of a laugh, a glint of cynicism entering his gaze, making it harder, darker. 'She asked to meet in private and offered herself to me.'

Allegra couldn't explain why she felt such a sharp dart of jealousy. What did she care who he slept with and why? She might care once they were married, but his past was his past, and it had nothing to do with her. 'What did you do?'

'What do you think I did?'

'Told her to get lost?'

'Wrong.' His eyes contained a gleam of malice. 'I slept with her first and *then* I told her to get lost.'

CHAPTER THREE

ALL THROUGH THE christening service the following day, Allegra couldn't stop thinking about the ex who had spurned Draco's proposal. She'd tried searching for information on the net, but there was nothing about him having been in a long-term relationship. How many years ago had it been? Had it been long before he'd risen to the top, while he'd been still making his mark on the world?

Was that why he had never fallen in love and insisted he never would? Was that why he only ever hooked up with women for short periods of time—because developing an attachment would make him too vulnerable? If he had truly loved the woman, then Allegra could understand how hurt he must have felt—especially when his ex had supposedly chosen someone because they were richer than him. It would have been a cruel slap to the ego for someone as proud as Draco Papandreou.

There were few men richer than him in Greece now. His empire was vast, not just the luxury yacht building, which was growing exponentially across the globe, but also property. He owned numerous villas, not just for his own private use, but also for lease to super-wealthy customers. He had a sharp eye for business and had rescued many from collapse, building them up over time and selling them for a massive profit. He rarely spoke in public about his humble background as the only child of a fisherman, but she guessed it was a powerful motivator to keep expanding his business empire.

But Draco was also an enigmatic man. He only allowed people so close and he never allowed anyone to manipulate or hoodwink him. He was a good judge of character, a fact she had witnessed first-hand when he'd warned her about her first boyfriend. He'd been familiar with the boy's family—this being Greece and all—and had told her she was wasting her time with someone who only wanted to date her because she came from money. *That* had stung. No sixteen-year-old girl with confidence issues and a body she hadn't quite grown into wanted to hear something like that.

But, unfortunately, Draco had been right.

The boy had crowed about how he'd bedded her and then joked about what a disappointment she'd been as a partner. The vernacular he'd used had made the insult all the more hurtful and shaming. It had taken her years to sleep with another partner. Years. And even the last time she'd had sex—which was so long ago she could barely recall what he'd looked like—she had worried he was judging her on her performance, filing away notes to laugh about with his friends in the bar later. Allegra had blamed Draco for it all because she had only gone after the boy after Draco's rejection. The boy's cruel taunts had seemed to echo Draco's ego-crushing dismissal, further shattering her self-esteem.

Allegra looked across the formal room overlooking the terrace where everyone had gathered for drinks to wet the baby's head. Her father was doing more than wetting his son's head. She had lost count of the number of glasses of champagne he had put away. Was he worried about this merger or relieved it was now all sorted? He looked happy—the happiest she had seen him in years. But then, why wouldn't he? He had his perfect little family now, and his left-on-the-shelf daughter of thirty-one was being married off to solve his business woes.

Elena caught Allegra's eye and came over, carrying Nico in her arms. 'I haven't had a moment to speak to you in private, Allegra,' she said, smiling broadly. 'I can't tell you how happy your father and I are about you and Draco. Your dad's been so stressed lately but since he heard you and Draco are getting married it's like a weight's been lifted off him. You *are* happy about it, aren't you? It's just, you've been a little quiet and...'

Allegra forced a smile. Acting had never been her thing but there was no time like the present to learn. 'Of course I'm happy. I'm just feeling a little overwhelmed. It's all been such a whirlwind.'

'Yes, but Draco never waits around for paint to dry, does he?' Elena said with a light laugh. 'I think it's so romantic he wants to marry you as soon as possible.' She glanced at Allegra's abdomen. 'I don't suppose it's because you're...?'

Allegra avoided her gaze and looked at the baby instead, stroking a gentle finger down his tiny petal-soft cheek. 'No. It's just...we both have work commitments booked in months and months ahead and there's only this small window of time available.'

Who knew she could be so good at lying?

'But you do want children, don't you?' Elena asked, handing Nico over for her to cuddle. 'I mean, when you're ready? It would be awful to miss out. I thought I was going to until I met your dad and accidentally fell pregnant. I still pinch myself, you know.' Her gaze went to Allegra's father across the room and she sighed. 'I still can't believe he married me. I didn't think I'd ever find someone to love me.'

But did Allegra's father love Elena? The question seemed to hang suspended in the air like a cobweb. Whether her father felt the same love towards his young wife as she did towards him was questionable. He'd wanted a male heir, and he'd wanted a malleable Greek woman who wouldn't question his authority and who would be content to stay at home and rear the children.

'I've not really thought much about having kids. My career has always been my baby,' Allegra said. She had never been the sort of girl to peer into prams or go gaga at the mention of a baby. Her career had been her entire focus. She had put everything before it. But holding little Nico made a cordoned-off corner of her brain wonder what it would be like to have a child of her own. Nico's tiny rosebud mouth opened on a yawn and he stretched his little body, one tiny arm with its starfish hand flailing in the air. She captured his hand and pressed a kiss to each miniscule finger, marvelling at the perfect little fingernails.

Elena leaned in to straighten the hand-embroidered christening gown that had been in the Kallas family for over a hundred years. Allegra hadn't worn it as an infant because the privilege was exclusive to sons, a tradition that had been another reason to make her feel an outsider. Draco had mentioned the possibility of a child but he'd been teasing. It made sense that he wouldn't want any permanent legacies from their short-term union. And why was she thinking about having babies with him, anyway? She was supposed to be keeping their marriage in name only.

Good luck with that.

'Will you be all right with him for a moment?' Elena asked. 'I just want to pop to the bathroom and change my breast pads.'

'Of course.' Little Nico wriggled again then opened his eyes, looked at her and smiled a gummy smile. Allegra felt a wave of love so powerful it was like an invisible fist grabbing her heart. This was her half-brother and she was melting like honey on a hotplate. What would she have felt if it had been her own flesh and blood? She tickled the baby's button-sized chin. 'Hey, little guy, who's been a beautiful boy while all this fuss is going on?'

Draco came alongside Allegra and, slipping his arm around her waist, offered the baby a finger, which little Nico grabbed with his tiny hand. 'It's hard to believe how small babies are—he's like a doll.'

'Yes,' Allegra said. 'I keep worrying I'm going to drop him. I suppose you get used to it when it's your own.'

'You're a natural. You look like you've been holding babies all your life.'

She gave a wry movement of her lips. 'Yes, well, I like the ones you can hand back. Do you want a hold?'

'No way.' He took a step back and held his hands up like stop signs, as if she were handing him a ticking bomb. 'I'm no good with babies.'

'Go on.' Allegra kept coming at him with the baby. 'You're a big macho man. You're surely not scared of a tiny, defenceless baby?'

Draco looked as though he was going to resist, but then his expression took on a resigned set. 'If I drop him, then it will be your fault.'

'You won't drop him.' Allegra came near so she could transfer the baby into his arms. The closeness of him stirred her senses into a swarm of longing. The fresh lime scent of his aftershave with its woody notes was intoxicating and alluring.

He took the infant, holding him slightly aloft, as if not wanting to get too close. But then Nico smiled and gurgled up at him, and Draco brought him against his chest and gently rocked him in his arms, looking down at the baby with a small smile. Allegra hadn't expected the sight of him with a baby in his arms to stir her so much.

'I've never been a godfather before,' he said after a moment.

'Nor me a godmother,' Allegra said. 'I'm not sure what sort of spiritual adviser I'll make. Sometimes I feel I could do with some spiritual guidance myself.'

'Don't we all?'

She angled her gaze at him. 'What? The invincible Draco Papandreou in need of advice? Wonders will never cease.'

He gave her a self-deprecating smile. 'You'd be surprised. It took me a long time to get control of my life. I almost lost my way a few times.' He looked down at the baby again, his smile dimming slightly. 'Especially after my father was killed. I suddenly found myself all alone in the world.'

'How old were you when your mother died?'

'Six.'

Allegra had been twice that age when her mother

had died and she still missed her terribly. How hard must it have been for Draco as a small child to lose his mother, only to lose his father a few years later? 'It must have been awful for you when your father died so suddenly. Who looked after you?'

'I looked after myself.'

She frowned at the cynical edge to his tone. 'But how did you survive? Didn't some relatives take you in?'

His expression reminded her of a suit of armour. She could see the outline of his face but only through a mask of steel. 'What few relatives I had were not interested in a fifteen-year-old boy with an attitude problem.'

'So what did you do?'

'I fended for myself.'

'How?'

His eyes took on a sardonic glint. 'You really want to hear some of the wicked things I got up to? I might shock you.'

'Try me and see.'

He glanced down at the baby and then gave Allegra an inscrutable smile. 'Not in front of little Nico.'

Allegra was frustrated he didn't trust her enough to tell her what his childhood and adolescence had been like. Was his tragic past one of the reasons he wanted to settle down now? It was all very well, her harbouring secret little fantasies about having a baby of her own but, even if Draco had wanted one, having a baby together would cause a whole lot of complications she could well do without.

She had acted for a number of women divorcing husbands from a different country, which made the care arrangements for children particularly complex, especially if the split was acrimonious—and of course many, if not most, were. It was a legal and personal minefield and one Allegra wanted to avoid at all costs. She knew enough about Greek men, and Draco in particular, to know he would not want to live apart from his child or children. He would want control. And he would do whatever it took to maintain it. Luckily, a baby wasn't part of the deal.

Nico began to get restless and, as if tuned in to her baby's needs by radar, Elena came back and took him from Draco. 'Time for a feed, I think,' she said. 'You two make great babysitters, by the way.'

Once Elena left, Draco led Allegra out to a shaded part of the garden near a fountain where the tinkle and splash of water cooled the warm atmosphere. 'There are some legal aspects of our marriage to deal with. Can you free up some time mid-week? I'll be in London tying up some other business. I'll set up an appointment with my London-based lawyer so we can sort everything out.'

Allegra had no problem with signing a pre-nuptial agreement. She had investments, property and other assets of her own she didn't want to jeopardise when it came time to divorce. But it was a stinging little reminder of the cynical mind-set he had about their relationship. 'Sure. Just give my secretary, Emily, a call and get her to put it in my diary.'

'I know what you're thinking. But I have shareholders to protect, and I'm sure you too have assets you don't want to see compromised. It makes things less complicated when we wrap things up.' He waited a beat before adding, 'It's not meant to be an insult to you, Allegra.'

'I didn't take it as one.'

He lifted a fingertip to the space between her eyes and smoothed away a puckered frown. 'Then why are you frowning at me like that?'

Allegra forced her facial muscles to relax. 'I always frown when I'm thinking.' She moved closer to the fountain and trailed her fingers in the cool water. 'It feels weird to think this time next week we'll be married.'

His hands came to rest on the top of her shoulders, his tall, strong frame standing just behind her. The intimacy of his proximity sent a rush of fizzing heat through her flesh. She had to fight the urge to lean back into his embrace, to feel the stirring of his body. 'Having second thoughts?' he said.

And third and fourth and every number this side of a thousand.

'It wouldn't matter what thoughts I had, though, would it? I haven't got any choice. I have to do this or watch Elena and Nico suffer.'

He turned her around and meshed his gaze with hers, his hands going to rest lightly about her waist. His gaze searched hers for a long moment, his expression containing a hint of a frown. 'I know this has been difficult for you. Your father's situation has made things far more time pressured than they could have been. Creditors are impatient people these days. But, in time, I hope you'll come to see this as a good solution all round. For you especially.'

Why for her especially?

Marriage was such an enormous step for anyone, even when the two parties loved one another. But when neither of them were in love, then how did that bode for them? Sure, some arranged marriages seemed to work well, but surely that was good luck, or maybe one or both parties became so resigned to their situation they decided it was more tolerable to love rather than hate.

Allegra had felt such intense antagonism towards Draco for so long, she didn't understand why she felt so attracted to him. Was it her frustrated female hormones playing perverse tricks on her? The more time she spent with him, the more she realised she had fashioned him in her mind as an archenemy.

Funny, but he didn't feel like an enemy when he touched her. When he looked at her with those black-as-tar eyes with their unknowable depths. He didn't feel like her opponent when he kissed her, when his tongue played with hers in an erotic mimicry of sex that made her blood sing full-throated arias through her veins. Nor when his hands cradled her breasts or held her lightly by the waist, as he was doing now.

His fingers tightened a fraction and he stepped closer—close enough for her to feel the need rising in him that mirrored the ache rising in her. His eyes went to her mouth in a sexily hooded way that never failed to get her pulse on the run. He lowered his head as if in slow motion, leaving her plenty of time to block the kiss if she wanted to.

She didn't.

His lips were dry and warm on hers, just a brush stroke at first—a light touchdown of surface rediscovery. But then he touched down again, once, twice, and on the third time something restrained in him escaped and his kiss became one of passionate heat and urgency.

The same hot-blooded urgency coursed through her

from her mouth to the very centre of her womanhood. The sexy glide of his tongue into her mouth made her whimper in approval, her arms going around his neck to bring her body even closer to the glorious hardness of his. Draco's hands came up to cradle her face, his head angled to one side so he could deepen the kiss, taking her on a journey of thrilling, pulse-thudding excitement as her need for him built to a level she would not have thought possible even a few days ago. She tangled her fingers into the thick pelt of his hair, her mouth feeding off his. His teeth nipped her lower lip and then his tongue swept over it like a salve. He did the same to her top lip, his nip and tugs so gentle, but they caused a tumult of sensations to rocket through her body and pool in a liquid, sizzling fire deep in her core.

'Hey, break it up you two,' one of Allegra's father's friends called out from some distance behind her. 'Save it for the honeymoon.'

Draco set her from him with a smile at her father's friend Spiro while keeping her by his side with an arm around her waist. 'How's it going, Spiro?'

'Not as good as things are going for you, I'll wager,' Spiro said with a wide grin. 'So, you two finally got together. He's a good catch, eh, Allegra? You must be feeling pretty pleased with yourself, landing a man like him.'

Why's that? Because I was rabid-dog ugly and left on the shelf and no one in their right mind would ever have offered for me in a thousand, million years?

Allegra ground her teeth so hard behind her smile she thought she would have to be tube fed for the rest of her life. 'Actually, Draco is the one who got the prize catch, aren't you, darling?'

Draco's smile set off a smouldering glint in his eyes. 'But of course, *kardia mou*. I'm the hands down winner in this union.'

Allegra's back teeth went down another centimetre. But thankfully Spiro moved on to chat to other guests who had come out to the garden to enjoy the shade and light breeze coming in from the ocean. 'You're really enjoying this, aren't you?' she said out of the side of her mouth.

'You know what Spiro is like,' Draco said, leading her back towards the house with a firm, warm hand in the small of her back.

'Yes, he's a man who thinks all a woman wants is a man with a big bank balance. I find it *so* insulting. A man isn't a financial plan. I know there are probably some women out there who are gold-diggers, but personally I would never marry someone because of his wealth. It's no measure of who he is as a person.'

He gave her lower back a circular stroke, making her legs feel as though someone had snipped her ligaments. 'I agree with you. But, on the other hand, the fact that someone has had the discipline and drive to work and accumulate wealth must demonstrate some admirable qualities, surely?'

Allegra gave a snort. 'I had a client a couple of years ago. She married a man who'd inherited a veritable fortune from his parents. He was the laziest, most obnoxious man I've ever met. He was abusive to his wife, both during and after their marriage, and he was so darn mean about supporting his own kids once it ended. Money does something to some people. It brings out the worst in them, and then people get hurt. I see it all the time in my job.'

Draco tucked her arm through his. 'At least we come to this marriage as equals, or close enough to being equals.'

'I would hardly call my wealth equal to yours.'

'Perhaps not, but we've both worked hard for what we've got, and neither of us would like to lose it.'

There were worse things to lose...

Like my heart, if I'm not careful.

Emily was at Allegra's office door before she'd even had time to put her tote bag away when she arrived back at work on Monday morning. She closed the door behind her and pulled out the chair opposite Allegra's desk. 'Okay, so give it to me. What the hell is going on? Do you have any idea how gobsmacked I was to hear you're getting married?'

'I told you—it's a marriage of convenience,' Allegra said. 'My father's got himself into a financial pickle and Draco is bailing him out with a merger.'

Emily's brow puckered. 'But how come he wants to marry you?'

Allegra dropped her shoulders with a 'thanks for the compliment' look. 'Apparently he wants a wife and I tick all his boxes.'

Emily made an apologetic movement of her lips. 'Sorry, didn't mean to suggest you weren't marriageable or anything. You're gorgeous, and any man with a skerrick of testosterone would be thrilled to have you as his wife. But you've always been so against marriage—which to be frank is a bit of an occupational hazard around here. You broke out in hives before Julie's wedding, remember?'

Allegra remembered all too well. It wouldn't have

been a good look to be in the bridal party photos with
red splotches all over her face and neck—but apparently it hadn't been hives but a reaction to the facial
she'd had the day before as part of the hen's party spa
day. Just as well the make-up artist had done an excellent job of disguising it with cover-up. 'That was an
allergic reaction—'

'I rest my case.'

Allegra rolled her eyes. 'Anyway, I've agreed because…well… I've agreed, that's all. I've known him
since I was a teenager. I used to run into him at cor-
porate functions and stuff with my father.'

*And proceed to embarrass myself with humiliat-
ing frequency.*

'But six months ago you were spitting chips about
how arrogant and up himself he was,' Emily said. 'Now
you're wearing his ring. Show me, by the way.' She
leaned across the desk to grasp Allegra's hand. 'Oh.
My. God. Isn't it gorgeous?'

'Yes, I couldn't have chosen better myself.' Which
made Allegra wonder if Draco knew her better than
she'd thought, despite his claim he'd selected the ring
at random. What else did he know about her?

Emily sat back down with a sigh. 'Gosh, I wish some
handsome billionaire would force me into a marriage
of convenience. *Is* he a billionaire?'

'Pretty close to it, I think.'

Emily leaned forward again, her toffee-brown eyes
suddenly full of concern. 'You sure you're doing the
right thing? I mean, you don't have to go through with
it, you know. You can always say no even as the priest
is asking you if you'll take this man and so on.'

Allegra couldn't say no, but explaining why to her

friend might make her look even more pathetic than she felt. She was ashamed about wanting to please her father at her age but there was no escaping it. 'I know what I'm doing, Em.'

'You said no sex, but surely you were joking?' Emily said. 'I mean, look at the guy. What's not to want?'

Allegra could feel her cheeks giving her away. 'I've told him it's a hands-off affair.'

Emily snorted. 'Like that's going to work. Did he actually agree to that?'

'Not in so many words, but he has to respect my wishes or—'

'Wishes, schmishes,' Emily said, eyes twinkling. 'You want him. That's why you were so cross about him that night in December. It was him you wanted, not that loser who didn't have the balls to show up when he'd been the one to ask you out in the first place.'

'I was cross with Draco because he seemed to be amused by the fact I was stood up by my date,' Allegra said. 'I didn't find it amusing. I found it humiliating.'

'What you found humiliating was Draco witnessing you being left high and dry,' Emily said. 'No girl wants a guy she fancies to see her rejected by someone else. It's not good for the ego. Speaking of egos—am I going to be your bridesmaid, or aren't you having one, since your wedding's so rushed and all?'

'Sorry, Em.' Allegra gave her friend a grimace. 'It's a really quiet affair with only a handful of guests on his private island.'

'His private island.' Emily grinned. *'No problemo.'* She slipped off the desk and straightened her skirt. 'But I expect a full report with photos when you get back from your honeymoon, okay?'

'Will do.'
'Where are you having your honeymoon?'
'On his yacht.'
Emily's eyes sparkled. 'You're toast.'

CHAPTER FOUR

ONCE THE LEGAL work had been seen to during the week, Allegra didn't see Draco again until the day before the wedding, when she arrived at his private retreat via a helicopter he had chartered to meet her at Athens airport. Her week had been a nightmare of juggling work, arranging a wedding dress and packing for their 'honeymoon'. Every time she even thought the word, much less said it, it made her pulse gallop. She knew he wasn't the sort of man to force himself on her. It was her own uncontrollable desires she was worried about.

Emily was right. How on earth was she going to resist him? Spending a week on a yacht with Draco was going to test her resolve like a chocolate addict standing in the middle of a chocolate fountain with her mouth open. She had no self-control around him. He only had to look at her with that black-as-sin gaze and her heart would skip as if it were jumping rope for England *and* Greece.

She had work commitments back home once the honeymoon was over, but apparently Draco had business meetings that week in London, so they would be travelling back together.

Just like a normal couple…

When Allegra arrived at the island it was like stepping into paradise. The eye-popping blue of the ocean with its fringe of sand on the villa side as white as powdered sugar was nothing short of stunning. The island was part of the Cyclades group and the andesite rocks, lava domes and prismatic columns of its cliffs and hills were geologists' eye candy. They were relics of the intense hydrothermal activity of millions of years ago and gave the islands, and this one in particular, a sense of timeless beauty.

But it was the villa itself that made her breath come to a slamming halt. It was eye-squinting white, built on four levels with an infinity pool that overlooked the pristine beach below. Gardens that looked like something out of a fairy tale surrounded the villa, and there were cypress pines everywhere, including a thick forest of them on the hills at the back of the island.

Allegra had expected Draco to meet her, as he'd arranged the day before. But only that morning he'd sent a brief text to say he couldn't make it. *Couldn't* or didn't want to? When she'd pressed the pilot for more information, he'd informed her Draco was tied up with something on the island which, considering a wedding was taking place the following day, wasn't such an unreasonable excuse. There was certainly a lot of activity going on for all that it was to be a small ceremony.

But when a woman in her late fifties came bustling out of the front door of the villa, welcoming Allegra in broken English, to her surprise she found herself feeling disappointed Draco hadn't welcomed her himself. What about his insistence they act like a normal couple in front of his staff?

'Kyria Kallas,' the housekeeper said. 'Kyrios Papandreou will be here soon. He is…how I say?…too busy?'

Allegra hoped it wasn't a foreshadowing of their future. She had never been important to her father. Work had always come first. Was she to suffer the same treatment by Draco? She might not want this marriage, but the idea of being so overlooked sent a shudder down her spine.

Allegra smiled at the housekeeper and assured her she was fine without him being there when he had so much to do. She found out the woman's name was Iona, that she had been working for Draco for five years and he was the best employer in the world. Allegra had trouble getting the woman to stop gushing about him. No doubt Draco's charm had worked its magic on the widow who, from what Iona said, he had rescued off the streets of Mykonos where she'd been left to fend for herself after her husband had divorced her, leaving her with virtually nothing out of a thirty-year marriage other than the clothes on her back. Allegra knew Draco was a financially generous man, but she hadn't seen him as the type to take in a homeless person and train them up to be his housekeeper.

Iona led her inside and showed her the wing of the villa she would be staying in prior to the wedding. It was a beautifully decorated suite of rooms with a marble bathroom complete with a freestanding bath with elegant gold taps and fittings. The furnishings in both the bedroom and sitting room were a lush combination of velvet, silk and brocade, and crystal chandeliers hung overhead. Allegra was no art expert, but the works on the walls were a mix of old and new, with a few pieces that looked like they were worth millions. The views from the windows were so breath-taking, she couldn't stop staring and wondering how anyone could ever get used to being surrounded by such beauty and the grandeur of nature at its finest.

One of the staff brought in her luggage and once he had gone Iona asked if she could press the wedding dress and any other clothes that needed attending to.

'That would be lovely, thank you.'

Allegra wandered over to the window overlooking the ocean and the gorgeous stretch of sand that sloped to the sparkling water below. Even though inside the villa was beautifully air-conditioned, the thought of a swim at the beach was so tempting she was rustling through her bag to retrieve her bathing costume before Iona could get it unpacked. She decided on her one-piece because she didn't feel like parading around in a bikini that was smaller than most of her underwear—a last-minute present from Emily.

There was a pathway with steps down to the beach that went past the infinity pool. Allegra decided against using the pool because it was so exposed to the villa. She didn't fancy the household staff watching her while she swam—or her version of swimming, anyway.

The sand was hot between her toes when she took off her sandals, and the sun beat down on her back and shoulders when she slipped off her light cotton beach poncho. The water was as warm as a bath and as clear as drinking water—so clear she could see fish darting away with every step she took. She went deeper and then did a shallow dive, her whole body sighing with pleasure when the water closed over her heated sticky flesh. It was like being baptised by nature, reborn and renewed by the elemental pulse of the water that had lapped this beach for aeons.

She swam back and forth, marvelling at the fish below her, and enjoying the sensation of the sun shining down on her back and legs after a miserable summer so far back in London. It was pure bliss to feel the water move over her body with every stroke she took, the sound of it splashing and the occasional cry of a seabird the only sounds she could hear.

Maybe she could get used to this sort of life—a week or two in London working her butt off and then coming back to this. To sun, sand and sea…and a sinfully handsome, sexy husband.

Draco came back to the villa, from seeing to an issue with one of his junior staff members at the staff quarters, to find Allegra had gone down to the beach. He could see her from the terrace, moving through the water like a mermaid, her long, black silky hair floating out behind her. His hormones shuddered at the sight of her. Her navy-blue and white one-piece highlighted her neat figure in all the right places—places he couldn't wait to get his hands on again.

He had only touched her breasts through her clothes and that had been enough to make him crazy with lust. She insisted their relationship would remain unconsummated, but every time he kissed her the message from her response was the opposite. He wasn't the sort of man to push a woman into doing things she didn't want to do, but everything so far told him Allegra *did* want him. Wanted him as badly as he wanted her.

He walked down to the beach and stood with one

hand over his brow, shielding his eyes from the sun, watching her slice through the water. But, as if she sensed his gaze on her, she stopped, stood upright in the waist-deep water and swung the wet curtain of her hair behind her back. She looked like a goddess arising from the depths of the ocean. The water droplets sparkled off her like a spray of carelessly flung diamonds, her creamy skin almost as white and pure as the sand.

Draco shucked off his jeans, T-shirt and shoes and walked into the water towards her. He would have slipped off his undershorts as well, but he decided to keep things in his pants, so to speak. Making love to Allegra with his staff watching from above was something he was keen to avoid. Once they were on his yacht and away from prying eyes, well, who knew what might happen?

He came closer to her and ran his eyes over her body. His flesh tingled, wondering if her hands and mouth would be as thorough as his searching gaze in the not-too-distant future.

Her eyes met his in a flinty lock. 'Is all your terribly important business sorted now?'

Draco placed his hands on her waist but, while she didn't resist, she stood statue-firm with her eyes spearing him like dark blue darts. 'Sorry, *agape mou*. I had an issue with one of my young staff. A homeless kid I took in a few months ago. He's having some problems with the rules I've set down.'

She blinked a couple of times and her whole body sagged as it lost its rigid stance. 'Oh…'

He moved his hands to her arms, stroking her wet skin cooled by the water. It was like caressing silk. Every cell in his body pulsed and strained to get closer to her. The blood pounded to his groin, his brain filling with images of him pinning her to the sand and getting all hot and primal with her. 'You can't be seen scowling at me the day before the wedding, *ne*?'

Allegra let out a breathy little sigh and stepped closer, placing her hands flat on his chest, making his blood roar all the harder. 'I'm sorry... I was just feeling a bit overwhelmed with it all. Is he OK, this employee of yours?'

Draco held her by the hips, his need for her closing the distance between their bodies like a bridge of lust. 'I found Yanni under the influence of something back at the staff quarters. I wasn't sure if it was alcohol or something else. I had to make sure, because he's got a history of substance abuse.'

She bit into her lower lip with her teeth. 'Oh, how terribly worrying for you. Is he all right?'

'Yes, but he's going to have one hell of a hangover in a few hours,' Draco said. 'I've got someone watching him and keeping him hydrated.'

'How old is he?'

'Sixteen going on thirty.' Draco grimaced and added, 'He's seen things you and I wouldn't dream of even in a nightmare. He's been living on the streets since he was ten years old.'

Her brow was as creased as the lines the wind had made in the sand. 'How did you come by him?'

'He tried to pick-pocket me. I caught him, and he fought like a demon, but then I realised he was sick with withdrawals from something. He was shaking and sweating and not in his right mind at all. He was barely coherent. I took him to a rehab centre and got him some help, but of course he relapsed as soon as he was released. You can't be on the streets and on God knows what substances for six years without having a struggle to get clean.'

Her brow was still slightly furrowed. 'So you took him in yourself? To live with you here on your island?'

'Yes, because he's safe here—relatively,' Draco said. 'This being an island, I can keep him away from the nightclubs and bars and seedy types who want to exploit him to do their dirty work for them. He's a good kid underneath all the bluster, he's just had some bad stuff happen to him.'

Her expression was thoughtful for a beat or two of silence. 'Did you spend time on the streets?'

Draco didn't like talking about the time after his father had died and he'd been left alone in the world. He had no money other than the pittance his father had saved which hadn't even covered the funeral expenses. It was a time he would rather forget because his life could have turned out so different—or ended altogether—if he had made some of the bad choices Yanni had made. Taking care of the teenager was a way of reaching back in time to be the sort of mentor he had found in his first boss, Josef.

'A few months. It was tough. I could have gone either way. But I managed to get out of there and make something of myself to honour my father.'

'How did you go from there to where you are now?'

'Guts and determination,' Draco said. 'And some luck. I got work down at the boat yard and the owner of one of the yacht-tour fleets took me on. I went to night school to finish my education and juggled a couple of other jobs to get some money behind me. I bought my way into the business and then bought it outright from Josef when he retired. I built it up and expanded it after that. I figured Yanni needs someone like Josef was to me. Tough but fair.'

Allegra gave him a lopsided smile and her hands slid up to link around his neck, bringing her body even closer to his until he could feel the cool, wet press of her breasts and the hot swell of her mound. 'I didn't realise you were such a nice guy underneath all that arrogance.'

Draco smiled and settled his hands on the sweet curve of her bottom, his gaze briefly dipping to the shadow of her cleavage. 'If you knew what I was thinking right now, there's no way you would ever call me nice.'

Her eyes shone with the same excitement he could feel throbbing through his body. Her fingers laced through his hair, her lips parting, and the tip of her tongue snaking out to leave a glistening sheen of moisture over them. 'Are you going to kiss me for the sake of any staff who might be watching?' Allegra's voice was husky, her warm breath wafting across the surface of his lips. She smelt of sun and salt and sunscreen, and something else that made his self-control throw its hands up in defeat.

Draco gave a mock 'let's get it over with' sigh. 'All right—if you insist.' He brought his mouth to hers in a kiss that spoke of the longing in his body. He explored the interior of her mouth, his blood rushing like a torrent at her response. Her tongue tangled with his, playing cat-and-mouse and hide-and-seek and I-want-you-right-now. He brought her as hard up against him as he could, his hands cupping her bottom until he could feel the intimate seam of her body. Never had he wanted someone so desperately. It was like a fire in his system, roaring through the network of his veins, making him zing from head to foot with sexual energy and demonic drive.

Her soft little whimpers drove him wild, so too the way her hands played with his hair, pulling and tugging until every hair root on his scalp tingled. Her mouth was wet and salty and he fed off it like an addict on a drug he couldn't resist.

He brought his hands up to stroke her breasts through the wet fabric of her bathers but that wasn't good enough for him. He wanted to feel those gorgeous globes of sexy female flesh, skin on skin.

He *needed* to.

He *ached* to.

Draco turned them around so his back was to the villa, somewhat shielding her from view. He slipped the straps off her shoulders as if he were unwrapping a gift. Allegra's breasts were neither small nor large but somewhere perfectly in between—creamy white with dark pink nipples erect as he was. He palmed them first, allowing her to get used to the slight roughness of his hands from working in his boat yard. She made a mewling sound when his thumbs rolled over her nipples, her mouth giving his sexy little nips and nudges that made his spine shiver as if sand were trickling down between his vertebrae. She caught his lower lip between her teeth in a little kittenish bite that made him wonder if he was going to jump the start like a teenager on his first sexual encounter.

He pushed her breasts upwards to meet his descending mouth, stroking his tongue around and over her nipple on her right breast, and then the left one, leaving them wet and peaking. Draco moved his mouth to explore the curve of her breast—the top side, the underside and the delectable space between. Allegra tilted her head back, her long hair trailing like black seaweed in the water behind her. She offered her breasts to him like a worshipper offers something to a god. He made the most of it. Beyond caring if his staff was watching from the villa. He subjected each of her breasts to an intimate exploration with his lips and tongue and with gentle nibbles of his teeth, evoking a panting response from her that thrilled every drop of testosterone in his body.

He was so hard, it was painful. But, as if she knew the agony he was going through, one of her hands slipped down between their jammed-together bodies and freed him from his undershorts. Her fingers were cool and firm around his length, stroking and squeezing him under the cover of the water. Not such a great cover, given the water was as clear as bottled water, but he was well beyond worrying about that.

He pulled her bathers down past her hips, slipping his hand down to cup her mound, letting her body feel the subtle pressure of his touch. She moved urgently against his hand, gasping against Draco's mouth. 'Please…' The cry sounded as desperate as he felt. 'Please. Please. Please…'

He traced his finger over her, teasing her with his strokes, finally slipping a finger into her hot, moist body, stroking the swollen heart of her until she came with a rush against his hand. He felt every contraction and ripple of her inner muscles, the sexy panting of Allegra's breathing delighting him more than he could have imagined. She was so responsive to him. What full-blooded man wouldn't be pleased about that? Nothing satisfied him more than giving a partner pleasure, but somehow Allegra's pleasure meant something to him.

Something he couldn't quite explain.

Draco withdrew his finger and held her while she recovered. Her cheeks were lightly flushed and it travelled all the way down to her décolletage in a rosy tide. She sent her tongue out over her lips again, her gaze a little dazed. 'That was…'

'Good?'

She pulled at her lip with her teeth, her gaze slipping out of reach of his. 'Unexpected.'

'In what way?'

'I don't normally… I mean I've never done that with a partner…'

He inched up her chin so her gaze reconnected with his. Allegra's blue eyes swam with uncertainty…or was it shyness, or a combination of both? 'The first time you've had sex in the water?' he asked.

She took a tiny barely audible swallow. 'The first time I've come with a partner present.'

Draco frowned. 'Really?'

She gave a self-deprecating grimace, her half-mast lashes screening her eyes. 'Yes, well, I can do it by myself, but as soon as a guy is there, pressuring me to get on with it, I just…freeze.'

To say he was stunned was an understatement. How had she put up with such an imbalance in her love life for so long? Or was it because of her first sexual encounter? The shame from being humiliated by some jerk who probably hadn't known how to make love to her anyway? Draco's guts roiled with anger at how she had been treated. She was responsive to him. Incredibly responsive, which meant she trusted him. Trust was an enormous part of sex, particularly for women, whose bodies could be so easily exploited by too rough a handling. He was all for a bit of athletic sex, but there was no way he would ever hurt or humiliate a partner during it, nor would he settle for anything less than mutual pleasure.

But, right now, his pleasure could wait.

He slid his hand along the side of her face, an unexpected wave of protectiveness sweeping through him. 'Listen to me, Allegra. You can trust me to always put your pleasure first. You can take as long as you need. Women are wired differently from men. A good lover will understand that and allow his partner plenty of time.'

Her smile was shaky around the edges and her cheeks still tinged with flags of pink. 'So much for the hands-off arrangement. We're not even married yet and look how I'm behaving.'

He brushed her wet hair back from her face, looking into her dark blue eyes almost the same colour as the ocean. 'This chemistry between us isn't something to be ashamed of, *glykia mou*. It's to be celebrated. It bodes well for a healthy marriage between us.'

She moistened her lips and her gaze flicked briefly to his groin. 'But what about you? Aren't you going to…?'

Draco shook his head. 'Not that I don't want to, but

the next time we make love it's going to be to consummate our marriage. And preferably we'll be alone on my yacht without half my staff watching from the wings.'

She sank her teeth into her lower lip. 'That hardly seems fair to you… I mean, things were getting pretty heavy there, just then.'

He took her hands in both of his and held them against his chest in case Allegra went in search of him. He could only take so much, especially from those silky little hands that seemed instinctively to know how to handle him. 'It's a man's responsibility to control his desires, at all times and in all circumstances. I want you. Make no mistake about it. I can't think of a time I wanted someone more. But tomorrow will be all the better if we wait.'

Her mouth formed a twist of a smile. 'Careful, Draco, you're starting to sound like our marriage is going to be a normal one.'

He held her gaze for a beat. 'In bed, it will be.'

Allegra walked back along the sand to the pathway leading to the villa with Draco's hand holding hers. Her body was still vibrating with aftershocks from the pleasure he had evoked. It made her aware of every inch of her flesh, as if all the nerves had been given steroids and were twice their size and three times as active.

How had it happened?

Why had she allowed Draco to touch her like that? He hadn't followed through to claim his own pleasure, so didn't that make her seem a little pathetic? Like that teenage girl she used to be? Her wanton response to him demonstrated her vulnerability. She was a fool to give him more ammunition. She was supposed to be resisting him. Rejecting his advances, not encouraging such intimate contact. Not only encouraging it but responding to it like she had never responded to anyone before. Her breasts felt fuller, more sensitive, her inner core tingling with the memory of his inserted finger. If she was going to shatter into a thousand pieces with the glide of his finger then what was going to happen when he made love to her fully?

What do you mean 'when'?

Allegra ignored her conscience. Her conscience could take a running jump off the nearest cliff and drown in the Aegean Sea. Her conscience didn't realise what it was like to be thirty-one years old and so feverishly in lust with a man she couldn't sleep at night without her body writhing in frustration.

What was wrong with having a 'married' affair with Draco? It was one of the perks of the deal. The *only* perk as far as she could see. Well, there might be a few more, but she didn't want to think about them just now. Perhaps sex could be fine as long as she kept her emotions out of it, which shouldn't be too much of a problem, because her emotions had never been involved before.

No. She was ready for this. More than ready. Her body deserved some excitement after the miserable drought it had been subjected to. It would make the prospect of getting married more palatable, knowing that as soon as they were alone they would be making love… No. *Having sex.*

Better get the terminology right from the outset. She wasn't a romantic. That was Emily's territory.

Emily was the one who dreamed of being swept off her feet and carried off into the golden sunset by a handsome prince. A fantasy that had so far done Emily zero favours.

Allegra was far too practical for all that nonsense, which was part of the reason why she had got to this age without falling in love. She had ruled it out. Put a line through the notion. She had always kept herself from getting too attached to the men she occasionally dated. She was a career woman through and through, but career women needed sex too, didn't they? They couldn't be expected to do nothing but work. It wasn't healthy. Balance was what she needed. A balance of work and pleasure, and how better to get it than to be married to heart-stalling, sexy-as-sin Draco Papandreou who would allow her to come and go for work and play?

Thing was… Allegra had a feeling she might want to play a lot more than work. And to come more than go—no pun intended. The thought of flying back to London, to dismal weather, traffic-clogged streets and difficult clients when she could have all this sunshine, white sand and water as blue as lapis lazuli didn't hold any of the appeal it used to, when she'd been desperate to get away from Greece after visiting her father and get back to her normal routine.

All the paperwork, the phone calls, the emails, the lengthy court appearances and the constant tension from dealing with difficult partners of distraught, angry or bitter clients…. Here all she had to listen to was the sound of seabirds, the ocean lapping the shore and the whisper of the wind in the pines.

When they got to the top of the path, Allegra pushed

back some wisps of salt-encrusted hair out of her eyes. 'I so need a shower.'

Draco's smile had a hint of devilment. 'I'd join you but that would be asking way too much of my self-control.'

A tiny doubt peeped out from behind the curtain in her mind… What if his self-control was only that strong because she hadn't done it for him? Down in the water, she'd been sure he would lose control and be swept away on a tide of passion just as she'd been.

But he hadn't.

He had stepped away from her as if they had innocently embraced and not been in the throes of making… Strike that. *Having sex*. Did it mean she would always be the one in the relationship with less power? The one who needed most, lost most. She saw it every day at work. Women who cared too much, loved or desired too much, lost out in the end.

Was she going to end up one of those women she privately pitied?

Draco's gaze went to the frown pulling at her brow before she could iron it out. He placed his hands on her shoulders and gave them a gentle squeeze. 'I know what you're thinking.'

Allegra screened her features. 'I'm hot and sticky and have sand in places I didn't even know I had places.'

He gave a soft laugh and stroked the back of his bent knuckles down her right cheek. 'Don't doubt yourself so much, *agape mou*. You have no reason to feel insecure with me.'

Like that's going to reassure me.

Allegra had never felt more insecure, more worried she was stepping over a vertiginous cliff into the unknown…or maybe not so much the unknown as the dreaded. Within less than twenty-four hours, she would be married to Draco Papandreou. She would wear his ring and share his bed and all his gloriously luxurious villas. But there was one truth she couldn't escape from no matter how much she tried to ignore it.

She would never have his heart.

CHAPTER FIVE

ALLEGRA PREPARED FOR her wedding day like any other bride, the only difference being that a knot of panic had settled in her stomach and, as each second climbed towards the time of the ceremony, the knot tightened, drawing all her intestines into a clotted ball.

Elena had flown in from from Santorini by helicopter first thing with Allegra's father and baby Nico, and was on hand to help her get dressed. Iona, Draco's housekeeper, was in her element, fussing over Allegra as if she were her own daughter. In spite of Allegra's reservations and nerves, she couldn't help feeling reassured by their cheery presence. They believed this was a romantic wedding day for the bride and groom and she didn't want to be the one to prick their bubble with the hatpin of honesty.

Along with Elena and Iona were a hairdresser and a make-up artist flown in specially, apparently at Draco's command. Allegra knew he was keen to keep up appearances, but it still touched her that he had gone to the trouble of organising their attendance. It might not be her choice to be married under such circumstances, but there was no way she was going to look like a fright show on her wedding day.

But that wasn't the only surprise.

The sound of the helicopter blades overhead announced yet another wedding guest arrival.

Not long after, Allegra was about to slip on her dress when there was a knock at the suite's door.

'That will be your bridesmaid,' Elena said, beaming.

'But I'm not having a—'

'Surprise!' The door burst open and in came Emily, carrying a garment bag folded over one arm. 'One bridesmaid arriving for active duty.'

Allegra blinked back a sudden rush of tears. 'Em, what are you doing here? I—'

'Don't cry! Your make-up will run,' the make-up girl said, dashing back over with a cotton pad, eye shadow and eyeliner brushes like an artist touching up her precious canvas.

Emily handed her garment bag to Iona, who bustled off to press the dress ready for her to put on. 'Draco called me at work a couple of days ago and asked me to come. He told me not to tell you as he wanted it to be a surprise.'

It was more than a surprise. Allegra couldn't understand why he'd gone to so much trouble, contacting her friend and workmate without telling her. But then he didn't know Emily knew their marriage was one of convenience. Had her friend blown it? Had Emily let slip she'd been let in on the secret against his express wishes?

Once the make-up artist had tidied up her face, Allegra clasped Emily by the hands. 'I'm *so* glad you're here.'

Emily grinned like a child let loose in a sweet shop with a platinum credit card. 'You should've warned me about Draco's wealth. I didn't realise you could have silver service on a helicopter. And he flew me first class from London to Athens last night and put me up in the most amazing hotel. I lost count of how many champagnes I was served on that flight. I felt like a movie star. That man has serious class.'

'Em…?' Allegra gave her a 'did you or didn't you?' look.

Emily's smile never faltered and she gave a covert wink. 'You should see the dress I've got. Actually, I've got three, so you could choose the colour you like best.' She went over to Iona who had hung the three dresses on silk-padded clothes hangers. 'Shell-pink, baby-blue or café latte?'

'The shell-pink,' Allegra said, turning to Elena, who was hovering nearby. 'What do you think, Elena? It would go best, don't you think?'

Elena nodded. 'Absolutely. It's perfect with the oyster silk white of your dress. Speaking of your dress— we'd better get you into it. We've only got a few minutes until the ceremony starts.'

Allegra felt like a royal princess when the girls and Iona helped her into her dress and veil. She had never had so much attention showered on her and she was surprised to find she was enjoying it. Having Emily there meant so much to her. Why had Draco gone to so much trouble? It made her feel that he cared for her. *Really* cared for her. Or did he just *really* care what people made of their somewhat hasty wedding?

Elena and Iona went ahead to take their positions on the velvet-covered and ribbon-festooned seats set either side of the strip of red carpet laid down in the formal garden.

Emily stayed to adjust Allegra's veil before they made their way out. 'You look amazing, sweetie. You could model for one of those bridal magazines.'

Allegra grasped her friend's hands again. 'You didn't let on that you know, did you?'

'No, but even if I took my contacts out I could see you're halfway to being in love with him, if you're not fully there already,' Emily said. 'Truly, he's something else to look at, isn't he? And that smile. Gosh, I'm halfway in love with him myself.' She winked. 'Only kidding.'

Allegra drew in a steadying breath and smoothed her palms over the satin of her figure-hugging gown. 'Are you sure I look okay? I don't look fat, do I? I bought this in my lunch hour and now I'm wondering if I should've—'

'You look a-maz-ing,' Emily said. 'That dress is perfect for you. It highlights everything I hate about you: your breasts, your hips, your bum—which is so tiny I wouldn't even classify it as a bum. Seriously, hon, you're going to pop Draco's eyeballs.'

Allegra adjusted the cleavage of her dress and grimaced. 'As long as I don't pop out of this dress.'

She stood at the top of the strip of red carpet with her father a short time later, trying to settle the hive of nerves in her stomach. While it was nice to have Emily here, and for Elena and Iona to be so kind and helpful, it didn't take away from the fact this wedding was not her choice. Not even marriage to Draco, the most attractive and sexy man she knew.

Especially because it was Draco.

He had too much power over her. Too much sensual power, which he had already demonstrated with stunning expertise. Seeing him in that sharply tailored suit and neatly aligned bow tie was enough to get her pulses racing. His dark-as-night gaze met hers and the edges of his mouth came up in a smile that spoke of triumph, rather than the emotion she hadn't realised till now she wanted to see.

But she didn't even like Draco. Of course she didn't… And marrying a guy who only wanted you to secure a much-prized business deal was a little lowering, to say the least.

'Ready to go?' her father asked.

'I could have done this on my own, you know,' Allegra said in a low tone so no one nearby could overhear. 'I don't believe in fathers giving away their daughters. It's positively feudal.'

Her father gave her arm a squeeze that was almost painful. 'Don't spoil it for me, Allegra. I've waited years for this day. I wasn't sure it was ever going to happen.'

She drew in a tight breath, stung by the partially veiled criticism in his voice. 'I'm only doing this for Elena and Nico. You do know that, don't you?'

'You should be grateful he was the one who won you,' her father said with a clipped edge to his voice. 'There were one or two other less savoury types who were interested but he outbid them with his offer of marriage. Hugely.'

A cold hand pressed on Allegra's spine. What did her father mean, Draco was the one who'd won her? *'What?'*

'Now is not the time to talk about it,' her father said. 'Ask him later.'

And then he led her inexorably towards Draco.

* * *

Draco had been prepared for Allegra looking beautiful. He had always known she would make a spectacularly gorgeous bride. And she didn't disappoint. She was a vision in an oyster silk slip of a dress that clung to all her assets like an elegant evening glove. Her simple white veil hung over her face and down her back in a floating cloud. Her hair was swept up in a coronet do that gave her the look of a princess that was nothing less than breath-snatching. He covered his reaction to seeing her with a smile that could have been termed gloating, but there was no way he was going to let her see he considered this ceremony as anything but a means to an end.

The deal was balanced firmly in his favour and he was fine with that. It was the way he did business and this was, after all, about business. He stood to gain the most out of getting her hand in marriage. Allegra didn't need his wealth or status because she had her own. He had played on her need to please her father who, in his opinion, didn't deserve it. Cosimo Kallas was a narcissist who was only happy when the attention was squarely on him. His wife Elena had been chosen because she was young and beautiful and attracted to him.

Just like you chose Allegra.

Draco shook off the jarring thought like he was shaking something off the back of his suit jacket. His marriage to Allegra was much more than that. He hadn't picked her from a line-up. He'd known her since she was a girl of sixteen. He admired her. He respected her. He *wanted* her.

And her father's business—and, more importantly,

her welfare—was a pressing issue that needed a solution, so here Draco was offering it. If he hadn't offered for her, another man would have done so with far more nefarious purposes. The business world was cutthroat and conscienceless. He knew enough about some of the rich and powerful creditors to know they wouldn't have thought twice about using her father's debts to force Allegra into their bed. If she thought being married to him was bad, he didn't like to guess what she would think about some of the alternatives.

This was his way of keeping them out of the equation.

It wasn't as if they would be living in each other's pockets. Draco liked that Allegra was independent, that she had her own career and commitments, because it would leave him free to see to his. He was prepared to be faithful because he didn't see any reason not to be during a short-term marriage. His father had instilled in him the trust needed to have a satisfying relationship. He had always admired his father for the commitment he had made to his mother that had continued long after her death.

And Draco knew the chemistry between Allegra and him was the best he'd ever experienced. He could only expect it to improve the more they explored each other. He couldn't wait for all this fuss to be over so he could get her alone and turn their marriage into a real one in every sense of the word. Allegra wanted him. Hadn't he proved that down at the beach? Their relationship would be one based on mutual lust.

The string quartet began playing 'The Bridal March'. Emily came up the red carpet first, but Draco couldn't take his eyes off Allegra, waiting at the end of the archway with her father, to begin the walk towards him. Had he ever seen a more stunningly beautiful woman? She looked like a bride from an old black-and-white movie. Her skin was luminous, her make-up emphasising the intense blue of her eyes, the aristocratic height and slope of her cheekbones and the pink perfection of her kissable mouth with that gorgeous beauty spot just above it. The silk dress moved with her body, making his hands itch and twitch to unpeel her from it and explore those delectable curves.

He drew in a breath but was more than a little shocked to find it caught on something in his throat. He'd always made a point not to be moved by weddings. They reminded him too much of his ex. Of all the hopes he had invested in that doomed relationship. Of his own calf-love foolishness. He'd been to a few over the years—friends' and colleagues' and business associates'—and he had never had his breath lock in his throat. It felt almost as if his whole life had somehow been slowly but surely heading towards this moment. That every road so far had led to this time, this place, this person walking towards him.

Allegra came to stand beside him and through the gossamer of her veil met his gaze. She gave him a trembling smile that plucked on a tight string deep in his chest. 'Hi…'

Draco had to clear his throat to speak. The uncertainty in her gaze, the slight wobble in her voice, made him wonder if she was experiencing the same unexpected groundswell of emotion. 'You look beautiful.'

The priest stepped forward with a broad smile. 'Dearly beloved, we are gathered here…'

Finally it was time to kiss his bride. Draco drew

Allegra closer and pressed his mouth to hers in a kiss that felt unlike any other kiss he had ever experienced. It wasn't because of the witnesses gathered or the solemnity of the occasion. It was a kiss that had a sacred element to it. A promise had been made and this kiss sealed it. Her lips clung to his, her hands resting against his chest, her right one over the thud of his heart.

Allegra smelt of summer flowers and her lips tasted of strawberries. He held her against him, praying his erection would cool it in time to turn to walk back through the gathered guests. He'd always considered it tacky when a wedding kiss went on too long. But now he wished he could freeze time. Stay right there and sup at her mouth until this burning ache in his flesh subsided—if it ever would.

He eased back to cradle her face in his hands. Her blue eyes shimmered as if she wasn't far off crying. '*Yia sou*, Kyria Papandreou,' he said.

She blinked a couple of times, as if to stop from tearing up any further. 'Thanks for bringing Emily here. It means such a lot to me. And for all the other... stuff.'

Was that why she was feeling emotional? The little jab of disappointment hit him under the ribs. Of course it wasn't about him. It was about her friend. He'd wanted to bring her friend here because Allegra no longer had a mother to support her and, besides, what bride didn't need a bridesmaid? He had asked his best friend to be his best man so it only seemed fair for Allegra to have someone she trusted and valued by her side. 'My pleasure,' he said. 'I thought she might hit it off with one of my friends from university, my best man—Loukas Kyprianos. He has a thing for English girls.'

'Even so, it was nice of you to go to all that trouble.'

He looped her arm through his and turned with her so they were facing the guests. 'Shall we let everyone get on with the party?'

It was a great party, Allegra had to admit, even though she spent most of it wondering about Draco's true motives in marrying her. She hadn't been able to get him alone to ask him to clarify what her father had told her. But it resonated with the sort of man he was. He might be ruthless when it suited him, but she knew him well enough to know he wouldn't stand for any sort of criminal behaviour. Who were the faceless men who might have blackmailed her into their bed if he hadn't intervened? The thought was too distressing to hold in her mind—like finding a cockroach in her glass of milk. It was revolting to picture herself with another of her father's business associates. Surely her father wouldn't have expected her to do it if Draco hadn't put his hand up and proposed marriage?

Why *had* he put his hand up? Could there be any other reason?

No. Why else had he said the marriage was temporary? Because he wanted to have her, but he needed an escape route, that was why. He'd been prepared to do the honourable thing by her, but promising to love, protect and provide for her for the rest of her life was a step too far.

Allegra looked around the party of revelling guests, her mind still in a whirling turmoil. It didn't take much for a gathering of Greeks to have fun when there was family, food and alcohol involved. Not that Draco had any family there. It struck her how alone in the world he was. He had friends and associates but no blood relatives. Weddings were times when families came together and celebrated with the couple.

She suddenly missed her mother with a pang that sat under her ribcage like a stitch pulled too tight. Not that her mother had really been there for her in the truest sense, but she ached for the mother she might have been if things had been different. But, strangely, she had a sense her mother would have approved of Draco. He was strong and disciplined, unlike her father, who had a tendency to live for himself rather than others. Draco didn't talk himself up, either. He did things in the background that one would ever hear of if he had any say in it. Would he have told her about the other men? He hadn't even told her about his commitment to Iona. His housekeeper had revealed it, not him. Iona had even told Allegra while she was helping her get dressed for the ceremony that Draco had set up a superannuation account for her with generous donations that set her up for a luxurious retirement.

Allegra stood with her arm looped through Draco's as various guests came over to chat. As if Iona could sense Allegra had been thinking about her, she came bustling over, cheeks pink from drinking champagne, and her eyes bright with happiness for her employer and his new bride. She grasped each of their hands as though she was making a pledge, her eyes going misty as they had during the service. 'Be happy. Be forgiving. Be friends.'

Draco leaned down to kiss his housekeeper on both cheeks. 'We will. I promise.'

Allegra waited until Iona had wandered off to talk to some other guests before she looked up at Draco. 'She's so lucky to have you. She told me she would've still been on the streets begging if it hadn't been for you.'

His arm went from around her waist to hold her hand, his thumb stroking the back of it in gentle movements. 'What she needed when her husband ditched her for someone younger was a lawyer like you. She had no one to stand up for her. She reminds me of my mother. She's a good woman, loyal and hard working.' He waited a beat. 'You rarely speak of your mother. Were you not close?'

Allegra grimaced. 'My mother never got over my brother's death. Losing him destroyed her. She gave up on life after that. My father would never admit it was suicide. He maintains the accidental overdose verdict the doctor put on the death certificate but I know she had given up. She simply couldn't go on.'

His hand cupped hers as if he was holding something fragile and precious. 'That must have been extremely tough on you, losing her under such awful circumstances. It's not as if your father is the nurturing type.'

'Yes, well, he wanted a son and heir, and when that son got sick he wanted another one to fix him, or—in a worst-case scenario—take his place,' she said. 'I turned up instead—female and an abject failure because I didn't have the right genetic make-up to save Dion or replace him.'

Draco's forehead creased into furrowed lines. 'But surely your father never said—?'

'He didn't have to,' Allegra said. 'I got the message loud and clear. Even my mother on a bad day would make it pretty obvious what a disappointment I was. That's why I was sent to boarding school in England so young. She didn't like being reminded of her failure to produce a healthy son and heir. I ruined her chances of falling pregnant again. She had to have a hysterectomy after my birth because I ruptured her uterus. I only found all this out when I was older but it explained a lot about my childhood. She wasn't the cuddling type, although there were plenty of photos with her cuddling my brother. She lost interest once he died and the only cuddles I got were from my nannies.'

Had she told him too much? Overloaded him with her Dickensian childhood drama? She rarely spoke of her childhood to anyone. Even Emily had only heard the cut-down version. She didn't like painting herself as a victim, but growing up without the security and comfort of parental love was something she carried like a scar. Mostly she could ignore it, but when she saw people interact with their parents, and in particular their mothers, the wound opened all over again. But she and Draco were alike in that they had both lost their mothers while young. If anyone could understand, it would be him.

Draco let out a long sigh and stroked the back of her hands with his thumbs, holding her gaze in a concerned manner. 'I've always been amazed at how well you turned out, given the tragic circumstances you were born into. But I had no idea you felt so unloved.'

And now I've signed up for a loveless marriage. Lucky me.

'To be fair, I think my father loves me in his way. Or at least, he does now that I've saved his precious business.' She met his gaze with a 'no secrets now' directness. 'He told me there were other men who had their eye on me. Why didn't you tell me that yourself?'

Draco's frown lowered as if he was thinking deeply and was troubled by those thoughts. 'I didn't want you to worry about it. I'd solved the issue as far as I was concerned.'

'It was an honourable thing to do...'

He shrugged as if they were talking about whose turn it was to take out the trash. 'I figured, better the devil you know.'

Allegra studied his unreadable expression for a beat. 'I'm starting to wonder if I know you at all. You're full of little surprises.'

'Don't read too much into my actions,' he said, expression still inscrutable. 'Your father isn't my favourite person in the world. I've always made excuses for him because the loss of a child is such a big thing. It's not the sort of grief you can easily move on from on. Although, he seems to have done so now.'

'Yes, his little affairs were his way of handling things,' Allegra said. 'My mother didn't seem to care what he did—she accepted it as normal. Even as young as I was, that used to really bug me. I often wondered if he'd stayed faithful to her would it have helped her heal a little better?'

'Maybe, maybe not.' He gave her hands a squeeze. 'Such sad talk for a wedding day, *ne*?'

Allegra gave a rueful smile. 'It's not like it's a normal wedding day, though, is it? I felt a little guilty acting in front of Iona. I hope she doesn't end up hating me for not being madly in love with you like every other woman on the planet.'

Draco's thumbs stilled on her hands as if they'd

been set on pause. His eyes held hers in a searching lock that made her feel that he was seeing more than she wanted him to see. Allegra's heart stammered. Had she given herself away? Shown how vulnerable she was to him? Not just in terms of physical attraction, but in terms of feelings she didn't want to feel but couldn't seem to control.

She couldn't fall in love with him. Couldn't. Couldn't. Couldn't. It would be unrequited if she did. He had locked his heart away and she had better not forget it. His reasons for marrying her were not just physical, but it didn't mean he loved her. He'd wanted to protect her. Any decent man would have done the same. The best she could hope for was the desire he had for her would last. But it was a fragile hope. A hope on a ventilator and a timer.

But then he slipped her arm back through his and smiled. 'Don't you have a bouquet to toss?'

CHAPTER SIX

THE SUN WAS setting by the time Draco steered his luxury boat away from the jetty on his island. Allegra stood beside him, a light wrap around her shoulders, and waved back to the guests standing on the jetty and the beach, including Emily, who was in proud possession of the bouquet.

Emily was standing a short distance from Draco's best man, Loukas Kyprianos, and Allegra could see the goggle-eyed looks Em was casting his way, as if she couldn't believe what she was seeing. On the handsome scale, Loukas was like Draco—*off* the scale. But, while Draco had a tendency to smile rather than frown, Loukas had a more brooding demeanour, hinting at a man who preferred his own company and kept his own counsel. Emily wasn't the sort of girl to get her head turned by a good-looking man, but she was a sucker for a man with secrets, given she had one or two of her own.

Draco manoeuvred the boat into the direction of the setting sun, which was now a fireball of red suspended on the smoky-blue plane of the horizon. A swathe of stratocumulus clouds reflected the burnished gold of the sun below and the grey and indigo bruise-like streaks of colour above.

A light breeze moved over the surface of the water, sped up by the passage of the boat. It played with Allegra's hair, which was already in two minds whether to stay up in her coronet do or give up and swing about her back and shoulders. She pushed the straying strands away from her face and resisted the temptation to slip her hand into Draco's outstretched one as he stood at the wheel.

He smiled down at her. 'All right? Not seasick yet?'

She shook her head. 'No. I'm pretty good on boats normally. Although, I guess I shouldn't speak too soon.'

'You'll be fine. The weather forecast is good.' He glanced back at the jetty. 'How's Emily getting on with Loukas?'

Allegra cocked her head. 'Are you trying to set them up or something?'

He gave a shrug. 'If it happens, it happens.'

'He doesn't look the type who needs a hand in that department,' she said. 'Who is he? He's seems familiar, but I'm sure I haven't met him before today.'

'He keeps a low profile—or tries to,' Draco said. 'We met at university. I was doing a business degree and he was doing computer engineering and software development. He's designed some of the most sophisticated security systems in the world. So secure, most government agencies such as MI5 and the FBI use his software.'

Good luck, Em.

'So is he on the lookout for a wife?' Allegra asked.

He gave her one of his crooked smiles. 'Not Loukas. His parents divorced when he was a young child and apparently it was one of those acrimonious, "use the kid as a weapon" ones. He doesn't talk about it and I know better than to ask. Both his parents have re-married and subsequently divorced, his father several times over. One thing I do know, he will never get married himself. It was hard enough getting him to agree to come to our wedding. You'd think I'd asked him to have a lobotomy.'

'Did you tell him it was a marriage of—?'

'No.' The tone of his voice underlined the word. 'We're close but not that close. No one is that close to Loukas. No one.'

Allegra chewed at her lip, watching the sun swallowed by the blue lip of the horizon. Why hadn't he told his best friend? Was it really because Loukas was a bit of a closed book himself? Why not tell his friend the truth? Or had he done it to protect her from anyone pitying her? 'I told Emily.'

'I know.'

She glanced at him in surprise. 'You do?'

Draco's expression was amused rather than annoyed. 'I figured you would. She's a nice girl. Seems to have her head screwed on.'

'Did you let on you knew she knew?'

'No.'

'I'm sorry, but I couldn't lie to her,' Allegra said. 'Everyone else, yes, but not Em. She would've figured it out anyway. She knows I'm not the sort of person to fall in love on a whim. But don't worry, she won't tell a soul. She's fiercely loyal and completely and utterly trustworthy.'

'Good to know.'

There was a little silence broken only by the slap of the water hitting the sides and hull of the yacht.

'Do you want to take the wheel for a while?' Draco asked.

'I don't know… I might run into another boat or something.'

'There's no one else out here. Come on. Stand in front of me and I'll steer with you.'

Allegra moved to stand in front of the wheel and he came in behind her, his arms either side of her body, his hands resting on top of hers where she was gripping the steering wheel. Who knew steering a yacht could be such a turn-on? The warm, hard presence of his body behind her made every nerve in her core jump up ready for duty. His broad hands almost completely covered hers, his fingers long, strong and so very capable. Deliciously, dangerously capable.

She could feel him against her bottom cheeks, the rise of his flesh an erotic reminder of what was to come. She shivered when he moved closer, his stubbly jaw grazing her cheek when he leaned down to help her navigate a larger than normal wave. The rocking motion of the yacht pushed her further back against him, sending her senses into overdrive. 'I want you,' he said.

'I would never have guessed.'

He gave a soft laugh. 'Minx.' He tongued the cartilage of her ear, the sensations rippling through her like waves. 'But then, I've wanted you since that night in London.'

Allegra shuddered when his teeth tugged on her earlobe. 'Funny, but I didn't pick up that vibe.'

He moved his mouth to the sensitive spot on her neck just below her ear. 'What vibe are you picking up now?'

'I'm thinking the honeymoon is about to start.'

He turned her so she was facing him, his eyes gleaming like high-gloss black paint. 'I need to drop anchor.'

Allegra linked her arms around his neck and gave him a sultry smile. 'I can think of something more fun we can do instead.'

He smiled and pressed a brief, hard kiss to her mouth. 'Go below and I'll be with you once I've got things up here under control…'

Allegra descended to the main cabin where a bar, sofas and large-screen television were located. There was a kitchen off that with a separate dining area, which wouldn't have looked out of place in a top-end-of-town restaurant. The master bedroom—one of four bedrooms on board—was big enough to sleep a football team as well as their support staff and sponsors. Maybe even some fans.

She was no stranger to luxury accommodation, but Draco's yacht was beyond anything she had seen before. Butter-soft leather sofas and ottomans, Swarovski light fittings and lamps and knee-deep, cream-coloured carpet. Polished timber woodwork and Italian marble in the wet areas such as the bathrooms. There was even a hot tub on the upper deck and a spa bath in the main bathroom. A bottle of champagne was in a silver ice-bucket with two glasses beside it, left by Draco's staff, along with their luggage, which had been unpacked and stored in the hand-crafted built-in wardrobes in the master suite. There was a supply of gourmet food in the fridge and pantry, both cooked and fresh ingredients, as well as a wine fridge with enough wine and champagne to host a cocktail party for a hundred guests.

Allegra couldn't look at the king-sized bed without a shudder of excitement. The same shudder of excitement she'd felt when Draco had said he'd wanted her when he'd run into her in London six months ago. She'd thought he'd been mocking her for sitting there so long, trying to make her glass of wine last the hour, trying not to check her watch and chew her lip and nails until they bled. But behind that glinting black gaze he had been sizing her up for himself. What had stirred his interest? Was it that he'd seen her as a convenient bride, a single woman on the wrong side of thirty who he'd assumed would stumble over herself with gratefulness when he offered for her?

But his motives had been far more honourable than that. Why had he done that? He was effectively saving her father's business and her, too.

Allegra sat down on the cloud-soft mattress and sighed. Why was she fussing over the fact he wasn't in love with her? People had sex without being in love all the time. It wasn't a prerequisite these days, even for marriage. Lots of people enjoyed a workable marriage with companionship and mutual respect holding them together. Romantic love didn't always last, anyway. The limerence period in a new relationship at best lasted two years. After that the relationship settled into the bonding phase…if it was going to, that was. Draco surely wouldn't let theirs go on for half so long?

It wasn't as if she was in love with Draco. But what if she succumbed to that lethal charm? She had already told him more than she'd told anyone about herself. It was as if her carapace had melted away. She actually liked him. As in *really* liked him. Liked his company, his smile, his dancing eyes, his body.

Dear God, his body.

The sound of his footsteps coming down to join her was enough to set her pulses off like thoroughbreds at the starting gate. Why hadn't she thought to buy some sexy lingerie? She'd been so determined to resist him but how long had that lasted? One kiss and she'd all but begged him to take her. One kiss! What if she was hopeless in bed? What if she couldn't orgasm with him? What if she took ages and ages, and he got fed up, and she had to pretend. and then she would be embarrassed and feel under even more pressure next time and—

The door of the bedroom opened and Allegra jumped off the bed as though she'd been shot out of a cannon. 'Erm… I think I'll have a drink. Would you like champagne? I feel like some, don't you? This is a good one. Wow… I've been to the vineyard. It was amazing, so picturesque.' She fumbled with the foil around the top of the bottle, sudden nerves and shyness assailing her.

Draco came over, took the bottle from her and placed it back in the ice-bucket. He put his hands on her waist, his expression as tender as she had ever seen it. 'You're nervous.' He said it as a statement, not as a question.

Allegra pulled at one side of her lower lip with her teeth, her cheeks feeling as if someone had lit a fire under them. 'It was probably a fluke down at the beach. I might not be able to do it again.'

He lifted her chin with the tip of his finger, holding her gaze with his. 'No one's keeping time here, *agape mou*. You can take all the time you need. We don't have to even do this tonight if you don't feel up to it. It's been a long day.'

'Don't you want to…?'

Draco's thumb brushed back and forth over her cheek like a metronome. 'Of course I do, but not if you don't feel in the mood.'

I've been in the mood for you since I was sixteen.

Allegra lowered her gaze to his mouth. 'I don't have any nice lingerie…'

He smiled. 'Do you really think I'd even notice? What I want to see is you. All of you.'

She shivered at the smouldering look in his eyes. The look that said 'I want you'. The look that spoke to her female flesh like the sun does to an orchid. Ripening it, opening it. Making it bloom and swell and release its scent. She placed her arms around his neck, moving closer so her body touched his from hips to chest. 'Make love to me…please?'

His mouth came down to cover hers in a kiss that spoke of deep, primal male longings only just held in check. Draco's lips moved against hers in a soft exploration, his tongue parting her lips with a gentle glide that made her skin prickle in delight. He courted her tongue, driving her senses wild with escalating need. She whimpered her desire into the warm, minty cavern of his mouth, her hips pushing against his with the need for more stimulation. His hands went from her waist to settle on her hips, holding her against his pulsing length. The eroticism of it thrilled her, awakening every nerve in her body, every sense on high alert.

Draco deepened the kiss with a bolder thrust of his tongue, a movement that made Allegra's inner core respond with a burst of feminine moisture, that instinctive, involuntary response that signalled her readiness, her eagerness, her desperation. One of his hands peeled away her dress as though he were removing cling film. It pooled at her feet and she blindly stepped out of it, her mouth still clamped to his. Her hands moved to undo the buttons of his shirt, her fingers struggling with the task in her excitement. With every button she undid, she placed her mouth to his skin, breathing in the intoxicating scent of him with that hint of lime and leather and late-in-the-day man.

He unclipped her bra and gently cradled her breasts in both his hands, his mouth moving from hers to glide down with blistering heat to her décolletage and over the upper curves of her breasts. The graze of his stubble made her insides clench with need, the glide of his tongue over her flesh evoking a murmur of approval from her lips. Draco's mouth opened over her nipple, drawing on it with light suction, the nerve endings responding with a frenzied dance of excitement she could feel right down to her core. He kissed the outside of each breast, then the undersides, and then her cleavage, his bristly face on the soft slopes of her flesh sending shivers of reaction all through her body.

Had anyone ever paid this much attention to her breasts in the past? Had anyone touched them with such gentleness? Cradled them and worshipped them? Treated them with such respect?

Draco's mouth came back to hers, subjecting it to another pulse-tripping exploration, his tongue mating with hers in a dance that made her ache for him become unbearable. She moaned her 'rescue me' plea into his mouth, her hands fervent, desperate on his body. She set to work on his belt and trouser fastening, sliding her hands over his flat abdomen, her palms and finger pads tickled by the prickle of his masculine hair.

He took over for her, shrugged off his shirt, unzipped his trousers and stepped out of them, his shoes and socks. Allegra couldn't help feeling touched he had left her knickers on until he was completely naked first. It showed a sensitivity she hadn't experienced with other partners. Only when he was fully naked did his hands go to her hips, gently sliding her knickers down her thighs so she could step out of them.

His gaze moved over her body, the desire in them ramping up her own. She pressed herself against him, her senses thrilling at the hard jut of his erection against her belly.

Draco moved her backwards towards the bed, laying her down and coming down alongside her, one of his hands on her abdomen deliciously close to the throb of her need. 'I don't want to rush you,' he said.

Rush me! Rush me!

Allegra was beyond words; all that was coming out of her mouth were breathless gasps and moans when his hand moved lower. She sucked in a breath when he brought his mouth to her belly button, swirling his tongue into its shallow pool until her back was arching off the mattress.

He moved his mouth down to the heart of her, preparing her by kissing her folds, stroking his tongue over her labia before separating her gently with his fingers and anointing her with his tongue in tantalising strokes and flickers that triggered an explosion of sensations that shook her like a rag doll. She bucked and arched and whimpered and cried as her flesh burst into a song that reverberated throughout her body until it finally subsided, leaving her in a languid, limbless state.

Allegra reached for Draco, stroking her fingers along his length, silently urging him to enter her body. After a moment, he eased back from her touch. 'What do you want to do about condoms? Are you on the pill?'

'I take a low-dose one to regulate my cycle.'

'Maybe we should use protection for the time being.'

It touched her that he'd given her a choice, not just gone ahead without consulting her on protection. He reached for a condom in a drawer beside the bed and sheathed himself. He came back to her, angling his body over hers so she didn't have to take his full weight.

That was another thing that struck Allegra about Draco. How many times had partners climbed aboard, so to speak, with little or no consideration for her comfort?

He smoothed her hair back from her face, his eyes dark and eager but with that element of concern that spoke of a man who didn't take consent for granted at any stage of the encounter. 'It's not too late to stop if you'd rather not do this.'

Allegra fisted her hands in the thick pelt of his hair. 'If you stop now, I'll never forgive you. I want you. Want, want, *want* you.'

His slanted smile made something in her stomach swoop. His mouth came down and covered hers in a drugging kiss that escalated her desire to another level that had her panting, writhing, wriggling to get the friction she craved. Finally, Draco came to her entrance, gliding into her with a smooth, thick thrust that made her gasp in relief and excitement. Her body welcomed him, squeezing him as if it never wanted him to leave. He moved his body within hers, deeper and deeper, gradually increasing his pace but making sure she was with him all the way.

Allegra was more than with him. She was a part of him. Consumed by the sensations ricocheting through her from the top of her scalp to the tips of her toes. Each thrust created friction against her, but not quite enough. It was like being suspended on a precipice, dangling there with the abyss beckoning. She whimpered and arched her hips, trying to position herself so she could fly.

Draco slipped a hand between their bodies and caressed her intimately, stroking his clever fingers over the swollen heart of her femininity until she broke free and flew and flew and flew. Fireworks, flashes, fizzes and floods coursed through her flesh. Her mind emptied of everything. It was as if, in those frantic moments, she'd become only flesh and feelings. Feelings that swept through her, flinging her out the other side just in time to sense Draco's final plunge.

He tensed above her, his breathing ragged, his guttural groan when he spilled making the surface of her skin tinkle and tingle with goose bumps. She held him during the short but savage storm, gripping his taut buttocks, holding him to her until he finally sagged as the waves of pleasure faded away.

Allegra couldn't remember a time when she had felt so close to another person. The skin-on-skin contact wasn't new, nor was having sex. The tangled limbs, and the sweat-beaded bodies and the crinkled bed linen were not foreign to her, either.

But the sense that her body had spoken to his, responded to his as it had responded to no one else, made her realise this wasn't just sex. What they had done was make love. Draco had worshipped her body, not exploited it. He had caressed it, not coerced it. He had respected it, drawing from her a depth of passion she had never given to anyone else. She hadn't been capable of it with anyone else. Her body had never wanted anyone like it wanted him. It was as if she was programed to respond to his touch and his touch alone.

Draco leaned his weight on one elbow and used his other hand to stroke her cheek. His eyes held hers in a gentle tether that made her feel even closer to him. It was as if he had glimpsed who she really was and liked what he saw. 'You were wonderful.'

Allegra gave him a shy smile. Silly to be feeling so shy after what they'd just done, but still. 'I don't suppose you've had too many complaints from lovers.'

He idly curled a strand of her hair around one of his fingers, the slight tug on her scalp making her shiver in delight. 'It's nothing any man should take for granted. What pleases one woman might not please another. Communication is the key and, of course, respect.'

She traced her fingertip around the sculpted perfection of his mouth, her core giving a little aftershock at the thought of the ecstasy his sensual mouth and potent body had given her. Pleasure she could still feel in every cell of her flesh like the echo of a far-off bell.

A thought suddenly crept up on her. What if Draco ceased to be satisfied by her? What if he became bored and went in search of someone else? She had witnessed first-hand her mother's shame at being shunted aside for a new mistress. It had made her mother even more depressed and disengaged from life. Allegra had often wondered if her father had been partly to blame for her mother's suicide by his inability to comfort and support her emotionally. She wondered if he was capable of doing it for Elena.

Draco smoothed a fingertip over her forehead. 'You've got that frowning look again. What's troubling you?'

Allegra gusted out a sigh. 'Nothing.'

He pressed his thumb pad on her bottom lip, moving it in a slow back-and-forth stroking motion. 'Talk to me, *agape mou*. It is good to communicate verbally and physically, *ne*?'

She couldn't quite meet his coal-black gaze and aimed for his stubbly chin instead. 'I guess I'm wondering how long this will last.'

He brought her chin up so her gaze meshed with his. 'This?'

Allegra licked her lower lip, tasting the salt of his thumb pad. 'Us. Having…sex. Don't most married couples drift into a less passionate relationship over time? What will you do then? Find someone else?'

A frown formed a bridge between his eyes. 'Didn't you hear me promise to be faithful above all others earlier today? While we're officially married I will be faithful, as I expect you to be.'

While we're officially married… Allegra searched his gaze, wondering, hoping, praying he meant every word. But how could she be sure? Didn't most people mean those vows at the time they spoke them? She was surprised to find *she* had meant them. She might not love him, but she still meant to honour the commitment as far as it was possible to do so. 'But our situation is a little different… We're not starting our marriage at the same place as other couples. What if you fall in love with someone? Someone you meet at work or wherever?'

His finger captured another tendril of her hair and began toying with it. 'What if you fall in love with someone?'

Allegra had trouble holding his penetrating gaze. She pushed out of his hold, swung her legs off the bed and reached for something to cover her nakedness. His shirt was the only thing handy and she slipped it on and crossed it over her chest without doing up the buttons. How could she fall in love with someone else when Draco was all she could think about? 'I don't think that's likely to happen.'

'Then why do you think it will happen to me?'

'Because it happens,' she said. 'It happens and you can't always control it. I represent so many clients whose partner met someone's gaze across a room and that was it. End of marriage. Most never thought it would happen to them. They thought they had a good relationship and then are suddenly left with the heart-ache of being rejected for someone younger and more beautiful. It's still easier for men to stray, especially when kids come along. It's hard work, bringing up a family, and some men can't cope with the focus not being on them any more.

'My father is a classic example. He got tired of my mother's depression after Dion died and got someone else on the side. Lots of them over the years—both she and I lost count. She was barely cold in her grave be-fore he parked a new mistress in the house.'

Draco got off the bed, pulled on his trousers and zipped them. 'Not all men are your father, Allegra. Your parents' situation was tragic. The loss of a child would test any solid relationship and your parents' relationship, from all accounts, wasn't solid. But don't paint me with the same brush. It's insulting, for one thing. And, for another, I'm not capable of the emotions you describe.'

Allegra frowned. 'But you're not incapable of feeling love. I saw the way you interacted with Iona. And I know you loved your father and grieved terribly when he was killed because you hate talking about it. Look at the way you put everything on hold yesterday to see to Yanni. You *care* about people, Draco. You care a lot. You might not call it love but many would.'

His tilted smile had a touch of cynicism. 'Yes, I care, and to some degree that could be called love. But as for romantic love? I did that once and it was the most foolish mistake I've ever made. I'm not going to repeat it.'

'What happened between you and your ex?'

He made a move to the door but she intercepted him and stalled him with a hand on his arm. 'Talk to me, Draco,' Allegra said. 'I've told you so much about my own stuff but you keep your stuff to yourself. I would like to know so I can understand you better.'

'There's nothing to understand,' he said, but she noted he didn't pull away. 'I was nineteen and full of the confident arrogance of youth. I thought she cared about me the way I cared about her. She didn't.'

A penny dropped inside Allegra's head. 'You were nineteen?'

Draco gave her a rueful look. 'Yes, right at the time you made that pass at me. I was still feeling a little raw. You got the rough end of it. Under other circumstances, your crush would have been a compliment, but instead it was a brutal reminder of the one who got away.'

Allegra bit her lip. 'I'm sorry. No wonder you were so…so angry.'

He brushed a finger over her lower lip as if to remove the sting of the bruising kiss he had pulled away from so long ago. 'It was wrong of me to take it out on you.' His hand drifted away. 'That was why I was so against you getting it on with that boy a couple of years later. I saw something in him that reminded me of my ex.'

And for all these years Allegra had hated him for it. 'But weren't you rather young to be thinking about marriage at nineteen?'

'For some people, yes, that would've been too young. But I'd been on my own since my father died,' he said. 'I felt ready to build a life with someone. Turned out I wasn't as ready as I thought.'

Allegra wondered if Draco would ever be ready to settle down for life after such a disappointment. His commitment to her was conditional. A two- or three-year marriage was hardly a lifetime commitment. No mention of love, just caring. How long was that going to be enough for her? 'I wish I'd listened to you about that boy. It would have saved me a lot of hurt and embarrassment.'

He gave her an on-off smile and turned away to shove his feet back into his shoes, before he reached for a T-shirt and hauled it over his head. 'I'm going up on the bridge to check on things. I'll leave you to rest or whatever. We'll have some supper once I secure us for the night in a sheltered cove not far away from here.'

Allegra's shoulders sagged when the door clicked shut on his exit. She was being silly. What did it matter if he didn't love her? Refused point blank ever to fall in love with her? They could still have a satisfying relationship. Far more satisfying than any relationship she'd had before. Sure, it wasn't the fairy-tale relationship she secretly yearned for, but how realistic were those yearnings anyway? She knew more than most about the sort of heartache that came from idealistic expectations in relationships.

This way was safer. They had a mutual desire for each other and were both intelligent and rational people with a lot more in common than most.

Besides, she wasn't in love with him.

And she would be perfectly safe as long as she stayed that way.

CHAPTER SEVEN

DRACO DROPPED ANCHOR and stood and breathed in the warm night air scented with the brine of the sea. He loved being out on the water, away from all his responsibilities, the burdens he had been carrying since he was a teenager, when life had seemed so hard and impossibly cruel. Out here he could breathe. He could reflect on the goals he had achieved instead of dwelling on the ones he hadn't.

He wasn't sure why he'd told Allegra about his ex, not in so much detail. But she had shared a lot about herself, deeply personal stuff that couldn't have been easy to share. He enjoyed being out here with her—maybe a little too much. The desire that roared between them wasn't something that was going to fade away any time soon. Not on his part, anyway. Draco didn't know what it was about her that made him so fired up. She was beautiful, but then, he had slept with many beautiful women.

No, it was more than that. She was captivating. She was smart and funny and she responded to him with such fervency it couldn't fail to delight him. Hadn't he always known that? Wasn't that why he'd been so hands-off with her for all these years?

But he wasn't hands-off with her now.

And that was something his body was thrilled about. More than thrilled. Excited, exhilarated, ecstatic. He'd had great sex before, too many times to count. But with Allegra something else happened apart from the physical act of sex. Something deeper. Her trust in him gave their intimacy a quality he hadn't experienced quite like that before. Her lack of experience was uncommon in a woman of her age and Draco couldn't help feeling pleased about it. It reeked of a big, fat Greek double standard but he was privately pleased she hadn't shared her body with lots of partners. It gave her relationship with him more significance, as if she had waited for him. What man didn't want a wife who was fiercely attracted to him? It would at least keep her from straying. If Allegra wanted him, then she would think twice about leaving the relationship before he was ready for it to end. Her desire for him was something he could rely on to keep her true to the commitment they'd made that morning.

But as for loving her...

Of course he cared for her, in his way. Care, concern, tenderness, love—weren't they much the same thing? But being *in love*, well, he wasn't going down that road again if he could help it. Draco wasn't such a cynic he couldn't see it worked for some people. People who were less guarded about their emotions. Less... disciplined. But he wasn't one of them.

Not now.

He had learned his lesson the hard way and had learned it well. Opening his heart to love had been foolish and immature and he had paid a high price for it. A price he refused to pay again. He could live a perfectly satisfying year or two with Allegra as his wife without the complication of emotions he didn't need or trust.

The word love was overused these days. People tacked it on to the end of just about every conversation like some sort of verbal talisman. But how often did they mean it? *Really* mean it? He only had to look as far as Allegra's father to see how little those words meant. Cosimo Kallas bandied those three little words around his new wife all the time, but how long before he found someone else to play with when Elena was too tired, or preoccupied with child-rearing?

At least Draco had the self-discipline to refrain from such peccadilloes. His father had set him a good example. Loyalty ran deep in Papandreou blood. Papandreou men stood by their promises even when it hurt. When they made a commitment, they saw it to completion, even if things got tough. He wouldn't have offered to marry Allegra if he hadn't thought he was capable of seeing the commitment through while they wanted each other.

It was a perfect arrangement for both of them. She was a career woman with no immediate plans to have children. He had his own work commitments that took him around the globe at a moment's notice. This way both of them could enjoy the benefits of an exclusive relationship until it was time to move on. What wasn't to like about her? She was beautiful and amusing and sexy and had a whip-quick intellect. He was tired of dating women who didn't have any conversation or little if no sense of humour. Tired of being feted like he was some sort of guru or celebrity.

Draco liked that Allegra saw him as her equal. Liked that she argued with him, debated with him, stood up to him. He had a strong personality but, rather than it intimidating her, it brought out the steely, uncompromising will in hers. He enjoyed sparring with her. Their verbal spats were as exciting as foreplay. He got hard thinking about her prim little mouth firing off another vituperative round at him. Telling him what she thought of him when he could read her body felt the exact opposite. He found it invigorating to interact with her verbally and, of course, physically.

Once he got the yacht settled for the night, Draco went back below deck to find Allegra in the kitchen sipping a glass of water. She had showered and was dressed in yoga pants and a lightweight, dove-grey boyfriend sweater that had slipped off one creamy shoulder. Her hair was still damp from her shower and was in a makeshift knot at the back of her head. She had looked traffic-stopping stunning that morning at their wedding, but his body leapt at the sight of her, even in such casual clothes and with no make-up on, her unfettered breasts outlined by the drape of her top, and his breath caught like a fish hook in his throat.

She put her glass down and raised her chin in that aristocratic manner of hers, as if they hadn't been writhing around naked and sweaty on his bed less than an hour ago. 'I hope you weren't expecting me to get supper ready?'

Draco smiled at the tiny spark of defiance in her gaze. After their little heart-to-heart she was pulling back from him, resetting the boundaries after their intimacy. Was she unsettled by the intensity of their love-making? If so, he knew the feeling. He could do with a little regrouping himself to re-establish the balance of power between them. Sex had a habit of tipping things in a relationship. Good sex, that was. And it didn't get much better than what they'd experienced together. 'Are you hungry?'

The tip of Allegra's tongue passed over her lips, her gaze slipping to his mouth for the briefest moment before her chin came back up. 'Depends what's on the menu.'

He closed the distance between them, allowing her enough room to step aside if she wanted to, but she stayed where she was, her dark blue eyes showing nothing of the tug of war her body was undergoing. But Draco could sense it. He could sense her arousal, the silent thrum of it moving back and forth like a radar signal between their locked gazes. The blood surged in his veins, his need growling and prowling through his body in response to the tempting proximity of hers. He glided a fingertip down the hinge of her jaw, stopping below her up-thrust chin, feeling the delicate quiver of her flesh at his idle touch. 'How about we start with a little appetiser?'

He brought his mouth down to the side of her mouth, the tip of his tongue circling her beauty spot, evoking a tiny whimper from her and a sway of her body towards his. He traced his tongue over her plump lower lip, following the delicate ridge of her vermillion border like an artist drawing a fine line. Allegra made another soft mewling sound, her hands going to his chest, the press of her palms inciting a rush of red-hot desire, making his legs tremble at the knees and his groin bulge and burn.

Draco moved his tongue to her top lip, sweeping it across the soft surface before taking it lightly between his teeth, a soft little 'come play with me' tug that made her press even closer, her hands fisting into his T-shirt. He cupped her bottom, drawing her hard against him, torturing himself with the feel of her soft curves against the pulsing hardness of his body. 'I want you.' Those were the only three little words he wanted to say. The only words he wanted to hear from her. The only words that mattered right now.

'I want you too.' Allegra linked her arms around his neck, opening her mouth against his, inviting him in with a flick of her tongue against his lower lip.

Heat roared through his body, his desire for her like a wildfire that had jumped containment lines. Every cell in his body throbbed with it. Vibrated with it. He kissed her deeply, exploring every corner of her mouth, breathing in the scent of her shampoo and body wash—the frangipani and freesia mix that so bewitched his senses. Her tongue tangled with his in a duel that made the base of his spine hum. Her hands tugged and released his hair at the back of his head, making him even wilder for her. The intoxicating mix of part pleasure, part pain ramped up his desire until it was a dark unknowable, uncontrollable force deep in his body.

Draco lifted her to prop her on the bench behind, stepping into the space between her parted thighs. Her legs wrapped around his hips, her mouth clamped to his in a kiss that was more combative than anything else. It was as though she resented her attraction to him, wanted to punish him for it. He took the kiss to a deeper level, thrusting his tongue into the warm, moist recesses of her mouth until she was clinging to him and making purring, breathless sounds of encouragement. Her hands clasped his head, her fingers digging deep into his scalp, but he enjoyed the roughness of it, the urgency of it. The thrill of having her turned on like a wild cat.

He pulled up her boyfriend sweater, accessing her breasts with his hands, holding them, cupping them, and running his thumbs over the peaked nipples. He sent his mouth on a tour of discovery, down the soft skin of her neck, the delicate framework of her collar bone and the scented valley between her breasts. He licked each one in turn, taking his time, drawing out the pleasure until Allegra was writhing, and pushing and grinding her hips against him in an unspoken plea for more.

He hauled her top over her head and tossed it to the floor, coming back to cradle her breasts in his hands, holding their silky weight, watching the waves of sensual delight pass over her features. He released them to pull off his shirt so she could access his chest, her mouth burning him, branding him with hot, damp little kisses that made the need in him tighten, tighten and tighten… He tugged at her yoga pants and she slipped down off the bench to free them from her body, leaving her in a tiny pair of black knickers with tiny hot-pink bows.

Draco picked Allegra up, carried her to the living area and laid her on one of the leather sofas. He removed the rest of his clothes and came down beside her, his mouth coming back to hers in a kiss that sent incendiary heat throughout his body. Her tongue wrestled and writhed with his, her lips soft, supple and playful. Her teeth got into the action with little kittenish bites that made the blood thunder through his veins.

It had been a long time since he'd worried about losing control but, with her mouth working its mesmerising magic on his, he seriously wondered whether he would go the distance. Need pulsed, powered and panted through him. Allegra's body beckoned to him, her legs opening, her arms around his neck as tight as a vine.

Draco put his hands to her wrists, encircling them like handcuffs, but she was so slender his fingers overlapped. 'I should get a condom.'

She pushed herself back against him, her breasts cool and soft against the wall of his chest, her eyelids lowered to half-mast like a sexy siren's. 'I'm on the pill. Make love to me. *Now.*'

That was another thing he hadn't done in a long time and then only the once: gone bareback. But in the context of their exclusive relationship he didn't have the usual list of reasons why he should halt proceedings to access protection. Allegra was taking contraception, in any case. He cradled her face in his hands, locking his gaze with hers. 'Are you sure?'

Her pupils were wide with desire, her mouth plump and pink from kissing him. 'We're married. And we're not going to sleep around, right? I'm clean, but if you need to get test—'

'Done,' Draco said. 'I was tested six months ago when I ended a fling. I haven't been with anyone since.'

Her eyes widened in surprise. 'No one? No one at all?'

He brushed an imaginary strand of hair away from her face. 'Seeing you that night reminded me of the chemistry we've always had. We have a passionate connection that's not just physical but intellectual. I decided that night I wanted you and, with your father's business worries taking centre stage, I soon came up with a plan to have you before someone else did. I had already been drip-feeding him money. What was a bit more to get what I wanted?'

Allegra rolled her lips together, her eyes shifting out of reach of his. 'It sounds a little…clinical…'

He brought up her chin with his fingertip. 'Does this feel clinical to you?' Draco kissed her softly, lingeringly, allowing her time to respond with the fervent passion he knew she couldn't contain. Her mouth flowered open, her arms going back around his neck, her soft little moan of acquiescence as sweet as any music he'd ever heard.

He moved from her mouth to kiss a pathway down between her breasts to her belly button, swirling his tongue around the tiny whorl of flesh before going lower. Allegra gave another whimper—part excitement, part nervousness.

He calmed her by placing a palm on her belly. 'Relax, *glykia mou*. I won't hurt you.'

She drew in a breath and he separated her tender folds, discovering her all over again. The secrets of her body, the scent and softness, the thrill of feeling her respond to his lips and tongue, was intoxicating to him. She arched up and shuddered as the orgasm powered through her in waves he could feel against his tongue.

She flopped back against the sofa cushions and he came over her, gliding into her with a long, deep thrust that made the hairs on his head shiver and shudder at the roots. Draco cut back a groan, but he couldn't slow down. Not now. Not now this urgent, desperate need was on the run. It broke free from his body, exploding out of him in a hot rush of relief that rained goose bumps all over his quivering flesh.

He was floating…floating…floating…all of his senses dazed into somnolence.

Draco stroked a lazy hand up and down the slim length of Allegra's thigh as if he were stroking a purring kitten. 'I hope I didn't rush you. Things got a little crazy just then.'

She shifted against him, her head tucking underneath his chin like a dormouse preparing for hibernation. 'No, it was…wonderful.' Her voice was as floaty as he felt. 'Truly wonderful.'

Draco looked down at her, pleased to see a curve of a smile on her mouth. He played with her hair, freeing it from its elastic tie, lifting it up and letting it tumble back through his fingers. 'We're good together, Allegra.'

She peeped up at him. 'The best?'

He gave her hair a teasing tug and then brought his mouth back down to hers. 'The best is yet to come.'

Allegra woke in the quietude a little while before dawn. The only sound she could hear was the gentle wash of the water against the sides of the yacht. Draco was sleeping spoon-like behind her, one of his arms over her waist, his legs entwined with hers. She had never spooned anyone before. It was such a cosy, intimate feeling to be curled up together, skin to skin. She listened to the sound of his breathing, feeling each rise and fall of his chest against the naked skin of her back. She glanced down at the band of his tanned, hair-roughened arm around her waist, the contrast of his darker toned skin against her creamy white making something tingle and shiver deep and low in her belly.

The curtains weren't drawn as they were so far away

from anyone in the private cove they'd anchored the yacht in the night before. The stars were like handfuls of diamonds flung over a dark velvet blanket, twinkling, winking, existing in a timeless and spectacular array. It struck her how long it had been since she had seen the stars in such magnificence. Her life had become so busy with work she rarely saw the night sky, other than in the city, where the light pollution all but wiped their brilliance out, apart from a stubborn handful. Allegra hadn't even taken holidays lately…not since her father had his cancer scare and she had used up all her leave, so the occasional star-gazing she did while taking a break had gone by the wayside.

Draco sighed and shifted behind her, his arm tightening around her body. 'Are you awake?'

Allegra felt the stirring of his erection against her bottom, sending a rush of physical memory through her body. 'I hope that's not your idea of foreplay.'

He chuckled and turned her so she was facing him. His dark eyes glittered as brightly as the stars outside. 'Here's the rule. You don't get to leave my bed until you've had a good time.'

Allegra traced the line of his smiling mouth with her fingertip. 'I'm having a very good time. Better than I thought possible.'

He captured her finger and kissed the tip, holding her gaze with the ink-dark steadiness of his. 'Not sore?'

She surreptitiously squeezed her legs together but wasn't quite able to disguise her wince when the overused muscles gave a faint protest. 'No…'

One black brow rose, demanding the truth. 'Not at all?'

Allegra caught her lower lip in her teeth. 'Well… maybe a little bit. That was quite a workout for me, given I'm a little out of practice and all.'

Draco stroked her forehead with such exquisite tenderness it made her chest feel strangely tight. 'I'm sorry. I should've thought and taken it more slowly.'

She lowered her gaze and went back to tracing his mouth, lingering over his lower lip and the rich coating of stubble below it. 'I guess I must seem a bit of a pariah, getting to this age without a healthy sex life.'

He inched up her chin again, his eyes lustrous and dark. 'I have enough female friends and colleagues to know how hard it is for a career woman to juggle work and relationships. Some men don't like not being the centre of a woman's world. Some careers are more demanding than others.'

'Yes, well, I had to fight hard to get where I've got,' she said. 'And, in spite of all the sacrifices I've made, I've still not made partner in the firm, nor will I be.'

'Is that what you want? To be made partner?'

For years, it was all Allegra had wanted. It had consumed her—the drive to achieve, to be recognised as competent and capable amongst her peers, especially the more senior ones. But lately her motivations had undergone a change. She still loved her job, but it didn't feel as satisfying as it once had. She found herself thinking of all the bad things about her work instead of all the positive things. 'I don't know…maybe it's time I shifted firms or something. I seem to have come to a bit of a career dead-end.'

'The glass ceiling?'

'That and other things…' Other things such as that niggling sense she was missing out on something.

Something far more important than a partnership in a law firm.

Draco threaded his fingers through hers and brought her hand to his chest. 'Ever thought of working over here in Greece? You could set up a consultancy of your own. You could help women like Iona.'

Allegra had always resisted the thought of working in her homeland. She had been so determined to be independent of her father. But she knew there were opportunities over here that would be career enhancing and personally satisfying. 'I'm still trying to figure out how I'm going to juggle my London job without taking on anything else.'

'I'm not expecting you to quit your job to cater to my needs,' Draco said. 'You have the right to work where you please. I have business commitments in England too. I'm just putting it out there in case you'd like to think about it.'

'What would be the point of setting up a legal practice I will then have to close once our marriage is over?'

His gaze suddenly seemed to be darker than normal. More intense. His brows were drawn slightly together in a small frown. 'Wouldn't you have had to leave when you wanted children, in any case?'

'Whoa there, buddy.' Allegra pulled her hand out of his and got off the bed to put some distance between them. 'How did we get from clever career moves to kids? You know my feelings on this.' Even as she was saying it she was feeling the opposite.

I want kids. I want them with you.

How had it taken her this long to recognise that niggling sense of dissatisfaction with her life was because she wanted a child? She had never seen herself as a mother, but since she'd been with Draco she couldn't get the thought out of her mind. But her pride wouldn't allow her to express it openly. How could she talk of her longing for a child when Draco had married her for all the wrong reasons? A child deserved to be born in love, not convenience. A baby was a blessing, not part of a business deal.

Draco left the bed and slipped on a bathrobe, the twin of the one Allegra had shoved her arms through and tied around her waist. 'What's the matter? I'm not insisting we have a child together. I'm just putting it out there for discussion. There's no harm in that, is there?'

'Why discuss it at all?' Allegra threw him a brittle glance. 'We're not staying married for ever. That was the deal, wasn't it? Why are you shifting the goal posts now?'

A muscle moved like a tic near his mouth. 'Let's drop the topic. It was a spur-of-the-moment thing. Forget I said it.'

'No. Let's talk about it,' Allegra said. 'It's obviously been playing on your mind. I thought you were only teasing when you first mentioned it. But you have no relatives to speak of. Most Greek men want an heir, especially men as wealthy as you. *Were* you teasing?'

He released a long, slow breath as if he were regulating his response. 'I was. But now I'm…wondering.'

Allegra wasn't sure she wanted to discuss it when she already knew what the outcome would be. They could have a child together but it didn't mean Draco would fall in love with her and stay married to her for ever. 'It's all right for you men,' she said. 'You don't have to interrupt your career to have a family. You don't have to give up your body for nine months, and longer still to breastfeed, and then spend years putting your aspirations on hold. You want the joy without the hard work.'

She was on a roll but she was spouting forth stuff she no longer believed the way she had even a few days ago. But she didn't want him to think her so willing to give up everything for him.

Not when he didn't love her.

But you don't love him, so why does it matter?

Allegra sidestepped the prod of her conscience. She didn't want to think about her feelings for him. It was dangerous to think about how he made her feel. She was confusing good sex with love, just like so many of her clients did. A couple of good orgasms and she fancied herself in love? Ridiculous. It was oxytocin— that was what it was. The bonding hormone tricking her into thinking she was falling in love with him. She was in lust with him. That was all. Lust. Lust. Lust.

'I'm aware of the commitment it is for a woman to have a child,' Draco said. 'But you're in a much better position than most women. With or without a husband, you could hire any necessary help, so your career wouldn't be compromised.'

'A nanny, you mean?' Allegra knew all about nannies. Nannies who came and went, who pretended they loved you and then moved on with barely a moment's notice after their affair with the husband of the house came to light. Nannies who made you feel wonderfully secure, only to rip that rug of security from under your feet so you were left in the inadequate care of a mentally unstable mother. 'No way would I allow a stranger to raise any child of mine.'

She turned away to straighten the bed for something to do with her hands, pulling up the sheets with a vicious tug as if she was putting the subject to sleep once and for all. She sensed him watching her and tried to relax her jerky movements, to control her body language.

But then she felt Draco come up behind her, his hands going to her shoulders and gently turning her to face him. His dark brown eyes were full of concern, not criticism, disarming her completely. 'This is a painful subject for you, *ne*? Then we will leave it alone. I don't want to upset you. I want to spend this week enjoying your company.'

Allegra was enjoying his company a little too much. How was she going to keep her heart out of this when he was so damnably attractive? She blew out a long breath. 'It is a painful subject. I hated being brought up by nannies. I would only just get used to one and then she would leave unexpectedly—mostly because her affair with my father had ended. He went through three or four that way. I'm sure that's why my mother didn't protest about me being sent to boarding school so young. She figured it would keep my father's affairs off site, so to speak.'

Draco squeezed her shoulders. 'Was boarding school tough on you?'

'It wasn't a picnic, that's for sure,' Allegra said. 'I didn't feel I belonged there. I was half-Greek with an accent that was nothing like all the upper-class English girls. I got rid of the accent as soon as I could and tried to fit in. But going home for holidays was just as hard. It was like culture shock. My mother couldn't cope with a child underfoot. I reminded her too much of Dion.'

His frown was so deep it drew his eyebrows into a single bar of black. 'Why do you think your parents didn't divorce?'

'I don't know... I guess because my father would have felt bad about leaving her after Dion died,' Allegra said, moving out of his hold to fold her arms across her middle. 'In the end she left him. I thought he'd bring home a love child well before this. But he didn't seem interested in marrying again until Elena got pregnant.'

'Elena seems happy with her situation.'

'Yes, well, she would be, wouldn't she?' Allegra said. 'She has a beautiful baby boy and she's married a man she loves. What's not to be happy about?'

His frown deepened. 'I thought you liked Elena.'

'I do—a lot,' Allegra said. 'She's sweet and caring, and has a lot of sensitivity, and heaps of integrity too. I just worry she might not be able to hold my father's interest in the long term.'

The same worries I have about you.

'Your father might finally settle down now he has his son and heir,' Draco said. 'But I see why you'd be concerned for Elena.'

Allegra rolled her lips together for a moment. 'You don't see the similarity?'

A flicker of puzzlement passed over his features. 'What similarity?'

'Between our situation and theirs.'

A muscle tightened in the lower quadrant of his jaw. 'No, quite frankly, I don't. It's a completely different situation. I've told you our marriage has a time limit. I promised to remain faithful during that time and, unlike your father, I am a man of my word. You have no reason to feel insecure with me. I might have a more colourful past than you but I have never cheated on a partner. Never.'

'But we're not in love with each other, so in a way we're worse off than Dad and Elena.'

Something shifted at the back of his gaze, as if he was reordering his thoughts. 'Perhaps we're not, in the romantic sense of the word, but in every other way that counts.' Draco held out his hand. 'Come here.'

Allegra came as if he had an invisible cord attached to her body, tugging her back into his orbit. He took her by the waist, holding her against the frame of his body, his eyes meshing with hers in a lock that made her inner core tighten in excitement. There was no way she could resist him. It didn't matter if he didn't love her. She wanted him anyway.

He cupped her cheek with one broad hand, his touch as gentle as if he were cradling priceless porcelain. He brought his mouth down in a feather-down kiss that stirred her senses into a stupor. Her lips clung to his. Need rose in her like a tide, leaving no part of her body immune. Her breasts tingled where they were pushed against the hard wall of his chest, her legs feeling as if they had seaweed for bones. Draco's mouth came back down to claim hers in a firmer kiss, his tongue entering her mouth in a sensual glide that made her insides twist and coil like kelp.

He eased back for a moment to look at her with eyes glittering with desire. 'Breakfast or back to bed?'

Allegra pulled his head back down. 'Read my lips.'

CHAPTER EIGHT

DRACO HADN'T HAD a holiday for months, so he kept telling himself that was why he was feeling so relaxed after a week sailing around the islands. He'd chosen a couple of private hideaways he was familiar with where he and Allegra had swum in quiet coves with the fish darting below them or had lain on pristine beaches.

But, if he were honest with himself, he knew it was because Allegra was proving to be the best thing that had happened to him in a long time. Maybe ever. He woke each morning with a tick of excitement in his blood. Not just because the sex they had was getting better and better, but because the companionship they'd developed had settled into friendship unlike he'd had before with anyone else. He looked forward to discussing things with her—current affairs or business things that came through on email. She had a good mind and sound common sense and he enjoyed listening to her take on current issues. They had cooked together, read together, walked, swam and snorkelled together.

And made love.

Draco couldn't quite bring himself to call it sex any more. Weird, because sex was supposed to be sex. It always had been in the past. But with Allegra it was

something more. Something more cerebral…even—
dared he say it?—emotional.

He shied away from the thought and where it was
leading. It wasn't love but physical bonding. It happened when the sex was particularly good. His body
craved hers. Hungered for her closeness. Got restless
when she wasn't nearby.

It was his hormones going crazy.

Nothing else.

Speaking of hormones, he hadn't returned to the
subject of children. He still wasn't entirely sure why
he'd brought it up when he had. When proposing, he
had brought it up as a test to see what her plans were
on the issue. But lately, he'd started to wonder if Allegra was projecting a cover-up opinion. He'd wanted
to make sure he wasn't doing the wrong thing by her
by tying her to a childless marriage. But she remained
adamant that having a family was not on her horizon.
It hadn't been on his either, but for some strange reason he kept thinking about it. He had no living close
relative. It hadn't used to bother him but now it kept
niggling at him. He was getting a taste of fatherhood
with Yanni and it wasn't always pretty.

Did he have what it took to be a good father? His
father had been a great dad. Hard-working and com-
mitted to him no matter what life had thrown his way.
But his father had been killed tragically and life had
been tough without a father to guide him. Tougher than
he wanted any kid of his to experience…

But if Draco suggested he and Allegra have a child
it would change everything about their arrangement.
Make it more permanent. The only trouble was…

He didn't do permanent.

* * *

When Allegra came up on deck the last morning of their trip, she slipped her arm around Draco's waist and smiled up at him before looking at the sun rising over the water in a golden wash of glittering light. 'So beautiful.'

He dropped a kiss to the top of her head. 'I think so.'

She looked up into his dark gaze and wondered how she had ever thought she'd hated him. The last few days had been some of the most relaxing and enjoyable of her life. She couldn't remember a time when she had felt more in tune with her body. Not just its sexual needs but in terms of general health and wellbeing. She had energy, she slept well and she woke up feeling refreshed and excited about the day and what delights Draco had planned.

But now Allegra was starting to dread the thought of going back to the real world. The world where work, long hours and difficult people sawed at her nerves, kept her awake at night and turned her stomach into a churning mess. 'Do we really have to go back today? Why can't we stay out here for ever?'

He drew her closer, his hands settling on her hips. 'That would indeed be a dream. But duty calls, I'm afraid. I've already had five calls from various staff members over urgent matters. I shouldn't have turned on my phone until after we berthed.'

Allegra toyed with the collar of his polo shirt, her hips resting in the cradle of his. Such intimacy seemed so natural now. Her body still leapt at his touch, her skin tingling and tightening when he gave her *that* look. The 'I want to make love to you and make you scream with pleasure' look that spoke to her woman-hood and made it do cartwheels, handstands and back-flips in excitement.

But, while the intimacy was fabulous, their communication could do with some work, especially over the last twenty-four hours. She had sensed a subtle with-drawing in him, as if he was only comfortable with being intimate sexually, but not emotionally. There was so much they hadn't discussed in any detail about their relationship going forward. Where would they live? Would he expect her to move in with him? He had bought a new townhouse in Hampstead a year ago. Her little house in Bloomsbury was her pride and joy. She couldn't imagine giving it up, as it was a symbol of her independence. The first place she had called home.

Her home.

She lifted her gaze back to his. 'We haven't talked about our living arrangements when we get back to London. Will you stay with me or at your place in London?'

'Most married couples live together. But I don't ex-pect you to move out of your home.'

Allegra wasn't sure what to make of Draco's an-swer. Did it mean he wanted to keep separate accom-modation? Why would that be? The doubts gathered like seagulls above a fishing vessel, circling her brain, looking for a place to land. Would he keep his house in London so he could keep his distance when it suited him? 'So you plan to keep your place as well?'

'It wouldn't be a sound business move to sell just at this moment,' he said. 'I've recently spent a fortune on renovating it. But it's not a decision I have to make right now. I'll revisit in a year or so.'

How could she know for sure if that was his true reasoning? A business decision not a personal one? Was it a get-out clause? A back-up plan in case things didn't go according to plan? Over the last few days Allegra had been lulled into thinking he was developing feelings for her. The way he talked to her, listened to her, laughed with her.

The way he made love to her.

Yes, made love.

It didn't feel like 'just sex' to her. Not the way he worshipped her body, made it feel things it had never felt before, made her senses swoon and her heart lower its drawbridge.

She had fallen in love with him.

Not at first sight. Not since she was a teenager, but by degrees. Each time they made love the feelings would intensify. There was no denying them now.

She had fooled herself into thinking he would fall in love with her. Sooner. Later. Eventually. But how long was too long to wait? What if it never happened? What if he wasn't capable of being open emotionally?

'So, where will we go once we get back to London?' Allegra asked. 'Your place or mine?'

Draco slid his hand up between her shoulder blades and then under the curtain of her hair, cupping her nape. 'I have to fly to Glasgow for a meeting later that day. I got an email a few minutes ago about it. I won't be back for a couple of days so you'd be best to go to your place. I'll catch up with you mid-week.'

Allegra thought they'd be flying back together but now he was shooting off to Scotland. But she refused to show her disappointment. It was unreasonable of her to expect his career to take a back seat when she had her own professional commitments that couldn't be cancelled at short notice. It had been a logistical nightmare taking this week off as it was. But it worried her this would be an on-going pattern of their future relationship. How long before his 'catch ups' with her became not weekly, but monthly, or even less frequent? How long before he went from looking at her with those glinting 'I want you' eyes to avoiding her gaze altogether, as her father had to her mother when he'd come back from a new mistress's arms? 'Okay,' she said. 'Fine.'

Draco inched up her chin, his gaze searching. 'I know it's not ideal. I wish you could come with me to Scotland but I know how hard it was for you to get this week off. It was the same for me. There will be constant compromises as we juggle two demanding careers. But we'll figure it out as we go.'

Allegra stretched her mouth into a 'I'm cool with that' smile. 'That's what you get for marrying a career girl. You have to share her with her ambition.'

His thumb pad stroked over her beauty spot, his eyes still holding hers in a penetrating tether. 'I have a feeling you're not as ambitious as you make out.'

She forced herself not to shift her gaze but to hold his without wavering. How could he know how conflicted she felt about her career? She had barely acknowledged it to herself. She hadn't even talked about it to Emily. She'd played the 'career girl' card for years. Work had always been her top priority. But if she interrupted her career path with a baby what would happen to her place on the ladder?

And did she even care?

Allegra slipped out of his hold and held on to the

side of the yacht. 'I haven't even got time for a pet. I really don't know how women do it—have a family and keep their career on track.'

He put his hands on her shoulders from behind, his body brushing hers with its warm, hard temptation. 'These things have a way of working themselves out, *glykia mou*. Your circumstances might be completely different in a year or two.'

Yes, she would be divorced and single again.

Allegra turned around, her arms automatically going around his waist as if she had no will of her own to resist him. But then, she didn't. Not one little bit of willpower. She leaned her head against Draco's chest, his hand stroking the back of her head in a soothing motion. What if her body decided for her? She was on the pill but it was a low-dose one and she was woefully lax at taking it. They had made love numerous times now without a condom.

What if she was already pregnant with a honeymoon baby?

But, even if she was, it didn't change the fact Draco didn't love her. Not the way she wanted to be loved. Totally. Unconditionally. Bringing a baby into a marriage that wasn't based on love would not be the best start in life for a child. Didn't she see that every working day? Children traumatised by their parents' arguing, or worse, marked for life with the memories of their care-givers at bitter war with each other, sometimes even after the divorce.

Didn't she bear similar scars herself? Her parents hadn't fought overtly with each other, but she had seen the stone-walling and cold-shoulder treatment from her mother and the pay-backs with affairs and long absences from her father. Was it any wonder she had issues with trust? Big issues?

Draco brought up her chin, his gaze meshing with hers. 'We need to set sail soon if we're going to get back in time for our flights out of Athens this evening.' He pressed a soft kiss to her mouth and drew back to smile lopsidedly at her. 'Back to the real world, *ne*?'

I can hardly wait.

Emily followed Allegra into her office first thing on Monday morning. 'So, how was the honeymoon? Good? Bad? Sensational?'

Allegra put her tote bag and briefcase on the desk and gave her friend a prim look. 'Since when have I told you intimate details about my sex life?'

Emily's eyes twinkled like fairy lights. 'You haven't had one for the last year or more, so how could you? Did you do it with him?'

Allegra slipped off her jacket and hung it on the hook behind her door, hoping her hot cheeks weren't giving her away. Every time she thought of Draco and the intense pleasure he'd evoked in her over the last week it made her blush from head to foot. 'Isn't that what couples on their honeymoon do?'

Emily plonked herself on the corner of Allegra's desk, swinging her legs like an excited schoolgirl. 'So what happened to the marriage of convenience?'

Allegra gave her a self-deprecating look. 'It seems I have zero willpower when it comes to that man.'

Emily picked up a pen and examined it as though it were crucial evidence. 'Yes, well, I'm inclined to agree with you, given his best friend is enough to make a ninety-year-old nun think twice about staying celibate.'

Allegra angled her head. 'Don't tell me you…?'

Emily dropped the pen and jumped down from the desk, her arms crossing over her body. 'I don't know what came over me—I swear I don't. I've never had a one-night stand with a guy. Never, ever.'

Allegra looked at her friend in surprise. 'You *slept* with Loukas Kyprianos?'

Emily winced. 'Guilty, your honour.'

'So, are you seeing him? Dating him?'

Emily bit her lip, the earlier brightness of her expression fading. 'He didn't even ask me for my number.'

'Ouch.'

'Yeah, big ouchy-ouch. I have terrible taste in men. Why do I always pick men way out of my league? No. Don't say it. I know why. It's because I have this ridiculous life script where the only man I want is the one I can't have. I think my mum is right—I need therapy.'

I could do with some myself.

'But it's only been a week,' Allegra said. 'He might still get in contact with you. He could get your number easily enough through Draco or me.'

'I'm not holding my breath,' Emily said. 'I may have sabotaged my chances with him anyway.'

'How?'

She screwed up her mouth and nose in a bunny-rabbit twitch. 'I talked too much. It was like that third champagne did something to my tongue. No wonder they call it truth serum. My mum would say it's because I was subconsciously inviting rejection. You know how New Age-y she is.'

'But what did you say to him?'

'I told Loukas I wanted to get married before I turn thirty in March and I wanted four kids and an Irish retriever.'

'What was his reaction?'

Emily rolled her eyes. 'You would've thought I'd asked him to propose to me then and there. I might as well have put a gun to his head and said, "Marry me or I'll shoot". Although it pains me to admit it, my mother is right. I sabotaged what could have been a perfectly good relationship.'

'I don't know about that,' Allegra said. 'Draco told me Loukas isn't the marrying type. His parents went through a bitter divorce when he was a kid. He said Loukas would never get married. He made quite a point of it, actually.'

Emily's shoulders sagged. 'I sure can pick them. I thought I'd learned my lesson after my disastrous relationship with Daniel.' She sat down with a thump on the chair opposite Allegra's desk. 'Sorry. I shouldn't be dumping all my negative stuff on you. Tell me more about the honeymoon. Are you in love with Draco?'

Allegra avoided her friend's gaze and sat down opposite, making a business of straightening her desk as though she had full-blown OCD. 'It's not that sort of marriage.'

'Like hell it isn't,' Emily said. 'You've been in love with him for years.'

'I had a crush on him, that's all—'

'Crush, schmush.' Emily's playful smile came back. 'You so do love him. Look at you. You're positively glowing with oxytocin.'

Allegra could feel her cheeks warming up like hotplates on a cook-top. 'Yes, well, Draco certainly knows his way around a woman's body... Thing is, am I going to be enough for him? He doesn't love me. He *cares* about me.'

Emily did her cute little bunny twitch again. 'Oh...'

'Not exactly what a girl wants to hear on her honeymoon.'

'No, but words aren't everything,' Emily said. 'Actions are what counts and it looks like you two have had plenty of that over the last week.'

'He's keeping his own house in Hampstead.'

Emily blinked. 'So? Aren't you moving in with him?'

'Why should I?'

'Because that's what brides do. They move in with their husbands.'

'But I don't want to move out of my house,' Allegra said. 'It's my home and I don't see why I should give it up just because my husband wants to live somewhere else. Women are the ones who always make all the compromises. And in the end they lose out. Big time.'

'You've been working in this job way too long,' Emily said. 'Compromise is the key to a successful relationship. Not that I can talk, as I've not had one, personally. But I live in hope.'

Me too.

CHAPTER NINE

ALLEGRA GOT A phone call from Draco later that evening when she got home from work. She had been waiting on tenterhooks all day for his name to pop up on her screen, the little kick of excitement when it finally did making her realise how much she'd missed him in the last twenty-four hours. 'Hi. How was your day?'

'Don't ask.' His tone was flat and jaded. 'I've got to fly to Russia in an hour. I'm at the airport now. I probably won't be back until Friday. Sorry.'

'Oh…that's too bad. Is it something serious?'

'Just business stuff.'

'You can talk to me about it, you know,' Allegra said with more tartness than she would have liked. 'I'm not some nineteen-fifties housewife who has no idea of how the real world works.'

He gave a rough-edged sigh. 'My client is a Russian billionaire who wants some face-to-face time over a design we're working on for him.'

'Couldn't you have sent someone in your place? You do have other people working for you, don't you?' Now she was starting to sound like a nineteen-fifties housewife.

'He's a difficult client,' Draco said. 'But his business is too valuable to compromise. I won't be away long—three days, five at the max. But enough about my business. How was it back at work?'

'Oh, you know, the usual stuff.' Allegra paused and added, 'Have you spoken to Loukas lately?'

'Not since the wedding. Why?'

'Just asking.'

'Just asking…why?'

She chewed at her lip for a beat. 'He and Emily got it on after the wedding.'

Draco gave a deep chuckle. 'Yes, well, I did tell you he had a thing for English girls.'

'He didn't ask for her number.' Allegra said it as if it was a personality defect.

There was a small pause.

'Was that a problem for her?' he said.

'A bit, I think.'

'She liked him?'

'She slept with him, didn't she? She's not the sort of girl to put it out for just anyone. Although she did have a bit to drink.'

'Loukas wouldn't have taken advantage of her, if that's what you're suggesting.'

'I wasn't,' Allegra said. 'She was keen on him but over-played it out of nervousness or something.'

'Over-played it?'

'She mentioned the M word.'

'Bad move.'

'Yes, it was apparently quite a dampener. Poor Em. She's such a sweetheart but she always falls for the wrong men.'

'Do you want me to have a word with him?' Draco asked.

'God, no. I think it's best if we keep out of it. We have enough problems of our own to interfere in anyone else's.'

Another silence ticked past.

'I mean…we have to sort out stuff, you know?' Allegra said. 'The living situation, for instance.'

'I thought we discussed that.'

'But what are people going to say when they find out we're keeping two houses in London on the go?' Allegra said. 'It's hardly the behaviour of a normal couple.'

'Then move in with me. Problem solved.'

'Why don't you move in with me?'

'Mine is a much bigger house,' he said. 'It makes sense to move in with me. You can rent yours out if you're not keen to sell it.'

'Why do I have to be the one who compromises?'

'It isn't about compromising, Allegra. It's about doing what's sensible.' Draco sounded as if he were talking to a child who had failed to grasp the simplest information.

Allegra wished she were still wearing her heels so she could dig them into the carpet. 'So far, I've made all the sacrifices in this relationship. You simply get on with your life as if nothing's changed.'

'Look, I have to go,' he said. 'I'll call you tomorrow.'

Allegra put the phone down and sighed. It wasn't the most satisfying way to end a conversation. But so far the only satisfying thing about their relationship was the sex. And even that was out of the question now, with Draco travelling thousands of miles away for days on end. Maybe she was being silly about the house. It made sense to use the bigger of the two. It was a big step for her, but not as big as marrying him. How could she expect him to fall in love with her if she kept harping on about silly little issues that weren't worth worrying about?

You expect him to fall in love with you?

Allegra chewed her lip until the skin felt raw. Was it too much of a dream to hope he would?

Draco leaned his head back on the headrest once he'd boarded his plane and closed his eyes, wishing he could close off his thoughts as well. Truth was, he could have sent someone else to Russia, but he needed some distance to sort out of few things in his head.

Why was everything suddenly so complicated? He had a filthy headache and a gut full of worry over Yanni back at home, who was giving his staff merry hell over being under house arrest. Now he'd upset Allegra over real estate. Her house was nice but it was practically a doll's house compared to his. Besides, he didn't want to live on her territory. He was the one calling the shots in their relationship. If he moved in with her, she would have the power to ask him to leave. He wasn't giving her that power, no matter how good they were together in bed and out of it. He could pack his house up and rent it out, but why should he? She was being stubborn.

Like you.

Of course he was being stubborn. Being stubborn was how you got things done. How you set goals and saw things through to completion. Being stubborn was how you built up a business into a global empire that was worth millions. Being stubborn was how you rescued a drug-addicted kid of the street and got him clean so he could have a life.

It meant Draco's life was a little more stressful than he'd like it, but that was the way things were. Allegra would come round. It was early days and she was still getting used to sharing her life with someone. As was he. This short separation would hopefully help him get some perspective. He had never been this close to another person. Not just physically, but emotionally. He looked forward to being with her, and he dreamt about her when he wasn't.

He had to rein it in. Draco didn't want to turn back into that callow youth of nineteen who'd fancied himself in love only to find it was a mirage. A fantasy. A dream built on air. He wasn't in love. His heart was in a straitjacket, where it belonged. He would miss Allegra while he was in Russia, badly. But it didn't mean he was in love with her. It meant he cared about her.

It was a mild word, yes, but the way he felt about her was anything but mild.

But when Draco got back to his hotel, from his third and final difficult meeting with his client, he sat in his suite and thought about how lonely it was eating yet another meal on his own. He could have gone out to a restaurant but the thought of dining out alone held zero appeal. No one to sit opposite him, challenging him, debating with him, smiling at his jokes and giving him those sparkly-eyed looks that signalled the same desire he could feel burning in his loins.

He missed Allegra. More than he'd thought he would. This time away was meant to give him some breathing room but instead it was stifling him. There was no trace of her perfume in the hotel room, not even on his skin. When he turned over in bed, the place beside him was cold and empty. That had never bothered him before. An empty space beside him meant he was free of emotional entanglements, but now it made Draco feel…well…empty. He'd tried calling her a few times but the time difference and the long meetings he or she had been in hadn't always worked in his favour. He'd been left feeling strangely out of touch with Allegra. Wanting her with an almost violent ache. Needing to see her like he needed his next breath.

He wondered if she was missing him. Did she stare into space and daydream about their honeymoon the way he did? Did she get a shuddery shiver all over her body when she thought about how they had made love on deck under the star-studded sky? Did she reach for him in the middle of the night and get a sinking feeling in her stomach when she realised he wasn't lying beside her?

Maybe it wouldn't be such a bad idea to move in to one house when he got back. A little bit of compromise wouldn't go astray, especially when it got him what he wanted—Allegra.

Allegra got back from court the following day to find a beautiful bouquet of flowers on her desk. She picked up the card and read the message.

Miss you. Draco.

Her heart gave a leap and she pressed the card against her chest just as Emily buzzed her on the intercom.

'Allegra, your stepmother is here. Have you got time to see her?'

Allegra put the card down on her desk. *Elena was in London?* Why hadn't she mentioned it at the wedding? Or was it a spontaneous trip? But that didn't seem like Elena at all. She was a homebody through and through. She didn't really enjoy travelling all that much and had said only recently how content she was to stay at home with little Nico. 'Sure. I haven't got anyone till four, have I?'

'No, you're all good. I'll send her in.'

Elena came in pushing Nico in his pram. Her eyes were red-rimmed and her face puffy, as if she had been crying. 'Sorry to barge in on you…'

Allegra came up to her and took her hands. 'What's happened?' She glanced in the pram to make sure Nico was all right but he was sleeping soundly. She looked back at Elena. 'What are you doing in London? Is Dad with you? Why didn't you tell me you were—?'

Elena shook her head. 'He's in Paris.'

An ice-cold tap began to drip down Allegra's spine. 'Paris? What for?'

Elena's bottom lip quivered. 'He's got a mistress there. I only just found out about her. He's been seeing her since I got p-pregnant.' The tears started in earnest then, accompanied by hiccoughing sobs.

Allegra hugged her close and stroked her back in soothing circular motions. What was her father thinking? He had what he wanted, didn't he? He had a son and heir and a loving and attentive wife. What more did he want? The selfishness of it appalled her. The cruelty of it made her stomach churn with anger.

Once Elena got some of her composure back, she

eased out of Allegra's embrace. Her watery gaze went to the bouquet of flowers on the desk. 'That's how I found out.' She pointed to the flowers. 'The florist must have got our names mixed up. I got this lovely bunch of red roses, and when I looked at the card it said "To Angelique, love always, Cosimo."'

'I'm so sorry.'

Elena turned a sharp eye on Allegra. 'Did you know? Have you known all along?'

'No, of course not,' Allegra said, shocked and more than a little hurt Elena would think it of her. 'Could it be a mistake? Another Cosimo?' Even as she said it, it sounded implausible.

'No, it's him,' Elena said. 'He didn't deny it when I called him. He ordered the flowers online for me and for her. He made some excuse about how he didn't want to pressure me for sex while I was pregnant. And here I was, thinking how kind and considerate he'd been when I was having all that wretched morning sickness. It makes me want to throw up all over again.'

Allegra wanted to throw up too. How could her father be so pathetic? 'What are you going to do?'

Elena's eyes streamed with tears and she brushed at them with the back of her hand. 'I want to leave him, but I've got little Nico to consider. If your father cuts my allowance, how will I afford a good lawyer to represent me?'

'I'll act for you,' Allegra said, handing her a bunch of tissues from the box on her desk. 'I know it's a little unusual, given he's my father, but I would never allow him to do you out of what's rightfully yours.'

'Oh, would you?' Elena asked, mopping at her eyes. 'Really?'

'Of course,' Allegra said, knowing it would be the end of her relationship with her father, but she no longer cared. Elena and Nico's welfare was a much higher priority.

Elena's situation was an unwelcome reminder of how much she herself had to lose. She was exactly like Elena—in love with a man who didn't love her back. He 'cared' for her. Like her father 'cared' for Elena. But at least Draco had had the decency to refrain from saying those three little words, unlike her father, who rattled them off all the time. And, unlike her father, he might be faithful to her for the duration of their marriage, but he planned to end it when it suited him.

He didn't love her.

That was the bottom line.

She would spend the next couple of years of her life—precious years she would never get back—waiting, hoping, praying he would fall in love with her. What if she had the baby she secretly longed for? She would be just like Elena, left holding it when he decided he wanted out. She didn't want to live like that. To be the sort of woman other women pitied. As she pitied Elena right now. If Draco couldn't say those words and mean them, then she had to make a choice.

'What are your immediate plans?' she asked Elena. 'Are you staying in London or flying home to Santorini?'

'I'm flying back to Athens to stay with my parents. I haven't told them yet. They'll be so disappointed but I have to leave him. I can't live with someone who doesn't love me enough to stay faithful. I just wanted to see you in person. I was worried you'd known about it.'

'I would never hide something like that,' Allegra

said. 'I'm appalled at Dad's behaviour. I'm shocked and sickened by it. I'm on your side in this. I'll get the paperwork drawn up and we'll take things from there.'

'I couldn't bear to lose Nico in a custody battle,' Elena said with a haunted look in her eyes. 'I'd rather die than face that.'

Allegra gave Elena another hug. 'I'm here for you every step of the way, okay? I can talk to Dad but I'm not sure it will do much.'

'No, please don't. This is my problem, not yours.' Elena took a calming breath and then gave a shaky smile that was a little off the mark. 'I'm sorry. I didn't even ask you how the honeymoon went. Did you have a good time?'

'It was lovely, thanks.'

'You're so lucky,' Elena said. 'Draco loves you. Anyone can see that.'

If only he did...

Allegra got home after a lengthy and arduous court hearing on Friday evening. She had only spoken to Draco a couple of times during the week, as he'd been in transit or busy with work commitments, or she had been in court and the time zones had made it even more difficult to connect. Besides, the conversation she intended to have with him was not one she wanted to have over the phone. She wanted to see him face to face. He'd arranged to meet her at her house. She had prepared a meal the night before and now she popped it in the oven to reheat before she showered and changed.

The doorbell rang as she was drying off her hair. The fact that he'd rung the doorbell was another reminder of how odd their relationship was. He didn't have a key to her house and she didn't have a key to his.

But then she didn't have the key to his heart, either.

Allegra's resolve took a punch when she opened the door to him. Draco looked as heart-stoppingly gorgeous as ever in an open-neck dark blue shirt and white chinos that showcased his olive complexion. 'Hi...'

He stepped over the threshold and took her in his arms, covering her mouth with his in a long, spine-melting kiss that made her resolve roll over and play dead. Her arms went around his waist, her hips flush against the potent heat gathering in his pelvis, her own body quaking with the need to get even closer. Draco pulled back to look down at her. 'That was a long week. Did you miss me?'

Allegra dropped her arms from his body and stepped back with a cool smile. 'I've been too busy to think about anything but work. How was your trip?'

His expression registered her response with a slight tightening around his mouth. 'Exhausting. I've crossed so many time zones in the last five days, I've got no idea what time to eat or sleep.'

'Come through.' She led the way to the sitting room where she had laid out drinks and some pre-dinner nibbles. 'Can I get you wine or beer or...?'

'What are you having?'

'White wine.'

'Half a glass will do.'

Allegra handed it to him with another impersonal smile. 'Here you go.'

He took the wine but put it straight back down on the coffee table. 'I have something for you.' He took out a package from his back pocket—a flattish square box wrapped in black tissue, tied with a gold ribbon.

She took it from him and carefully untied the ribbon and tissue to find a jeweller's box with a sapphire-and-diamond pendant inside. It was a delicate and elegant setting, almost simple in design, but the brilliant blue of the sapphire and the tiny sparkling diamonds that surrounded it made it one of the most beautiful pieces of jewellery she had ever seen. 'It's…gorgeous…' She glanced up at him. 'Thank you. It was very thoughtful of you.'

'Glad you like it,' Draco said with a smile. 'The sapphire reminded me of your eyes.' He took the box back from her. 'Here, let me put it on for you.'

Allegra turned around and lifted her hair out of the way while he looped the fine gold chain around her neck and fastened the clasp. The brush of his fingers against her skin made her whole body shiver in reaction. She turned back around to face him, her fingers absently playing with the sapphire. 'Thanks for the flowers, by the way.'

He placed his hands on her shoulders and meshed his gaze with hers. 'Why don't you tell me what's troubling you?'

Allegra pressed her lips together for a moment. 'I had a visit from Elena today.'

'Here? In London?'

She nodded. 'She flew over to talk to me face to face.'

'About…?'

'About my father's mistress in Paris.'

Draco's brows snapped together. 'He has a mistress? Already?'

Allegra slipped out of his hold and stood some distance from him with her arms crossed over her body, her hands cupping her elbows. 'Yes. Her name is Angelique. He sent flowers to her and Elena but the florist must have got the messages mixed up.'

He shook his head as if the situation was beyond belief. 'He's a fool. A damn fool. What's she going to do?'

'She's leaving him,' Allegra said, keeping her gaze steady on his. 'She says she can't live with a man who doesn't love her enough to stay faithful. I agree with her. You can't make someone love you—they either love you or they don't.'

There was a beat or two of pregnant silence.

'Allegra…' Her name came out on a heavy sigh that had 'don't do this' written all over it.

'I've been thinking this week while you've been away,' Allegra said, refusing to be daunted now she had made up her mind. 'This is how it's always going to be, isn't it? You don't love me. Not the way I want to be loved. The way most women want to be loved. The way Elena wants to be loved. I want love I can rely on, no matter what. Caring isn't enough for me, Draco. Flowers and expensive gifts and great sex aren't enough. I want you to love me. But, because you don't, our marriage has to end.'

He let out a harsh breath. 'Don't be ridiculous, *agape mou*. You're being—'

'You keep calling me your "love" but I'm not, am I?' she said. 'They're empty words. I want more than that. I deserve more than that.'

'Look, you're feeling let down about your father's behaviour and it's colouring your—'

'This has nothing to do with my father,' Allegra said. 'This is to do with us. But we're not an 'us', are we? Not in the true sense. We've married for all the wrong reasons and I can't be in a marriage like that. It will be like living my childhood all over again. Never feeling good enough. Never feeling enough, period.'

His brows came together over his eyes. 'You're not suggesting I'd carry on like your father? I told you I'd remain faithful. I promised you that.'

Allegra shook her head at him. 'Being faithful isn't enough. I can't be in a relationship that has a time limit. Every day that passes is a day closer to the one when you'll tell me you want out. That's not how a marriage should be. Even if you're not unfaithful, you could still fall in love with someone else, because without a solid commitment to me it leaves the door wide open for it.'

'I'm not going to fall in love with someone.'

'It's just as bad if you've ruled love out completely. I can't spend the next couple of years of my life hoping you will change. It's better to end it now. Before—'

'What about your father? The ink is barely dry on the deal.'

'You know something? Right now I don't give a fat fig if my father loses everything,' Allegra said. 'He deserves to lose everything, including his wife and son. I'm not going to be the sacrificial lamb for him. I've done it all my life. Papered over the cracks he made in my mother's and my life. I spent years compensating for his inadequacies but I'm sick of it. I'm reclaiming my life as of now, and it doesn't include you, because of the reasons I've stated.'

Draco showed no emotion. It was as if a curtain had

come down on the stage of his face. Allegra kept hoping he would say something…the words she so desperately wanted to hear…even though, if he did, she knew she would doubt their veracity. But why didn't he say them? What was so hard about saying 'I love you'?

'Is this about our living arrangements?' he said. 'If so, we can talk about a compromise. I was going to suggest it anyway, so…'

Allegra shook her head. 'Living together isn't going to solve this, Draco. Surely you can see that? We want completely different things out of life. Ultimately, you want your freedom and I want… I want a baby. A family.' There, she'd said it. Finally admitted the yearning that had been simmering inside her for the last few days. Maybe even longer…maybe since that night in London last December.

He flinched in shock. 'A baby? But you've always said you didn't want—'

'I know what I said but I've changed my mind.'

'Then let's have a baby,' he said, blowing out a breath as if everything was sorted. 'If that's the only issue, then it's easily solved. We'll have a baby and—'

'No,' Allegra said. 'I'm not having a baby to prop up a marriage that isn't working.'

'What do you mean it isn't working?' His gaze was forceful. Direct. 'Last time I looked, it was working just fine.'

'It's not working for me,' Allegra said. 'I'm not going to be second best, Draco. I want to come first. I deserve to be loved for who I am, not for what I can do. That was the script of my childhood; I don't want to follow it in adulthood.'

His expression returned to its inscrutable mask, all

except for a pulse at the base of his throat that seemed to be working a little overtime. 'Is this your final decision?'

Allegra set her chin at a determined height, even though everything in her was slumping, collapsing in despair. Why wasn't he saying it?

Tell me you love me. Tell me you don't want to lose me. Tell me. Tell me. Tell me.

'Yes.'

He gave a slow nod. 'We obviously can't get the marriage annulled.'

'No...'

'It will be embarrassing for both of us for a while,' he said. 'I won't speak to the press and I'd appreciate it if you didn't either.'

'Of course.' Why was he being so damn businesslike about it? So clinical and so composed, as if he wasn't ripping her heart out of her chest with his bare hands. Didn't that prove how little he cared? 'Erm...do you want this back?' Allegra touched the pendant around her neck. 'And the rings?'

'No. Keep them.' Draco's lips barely moved as he spoke, as if he resented the effort.

Allegra swallowed a puffer fish of sadness, but by some miracle she stopped herself from tearing up. Her eyes remained dry and focussed on his. 'I guess that's it, then.' She waved a hand towards the dining room. 'You could stay for dinner but I expect you'd—'

'No.'

'Right.'

There was another silence so acute Allegra was sure she could hear her heart beating. Boom. Boom. Boom.

'I'll see myself out.'

Allegra nodded, not sure she could take much more without showing the devastation she was feeling. Why wasn't he putting up more of a fight? Why wasn't he arguing his corner as he usually did? All he had to do was take her in his arms and show her what he found so difficult to say. Why was Draco walking away?

Because he doesn't love you.

CHAPTER TEN

DRACO WALKED OUT of Allegra's house as if he was on autopilot. His emotions were in lockdown. Emotions he hadn't known he had. He couldn't think past the thought of her pulling the plug on their marriage. He'd been blindsided. Again. What sort of fool was he to have fallen for it? He'd thought it was going so well. Why was she doing this? Why now, after that wonderful week away together?

All this talk of love… He hadn't said those words to anyone since he'd said them to his ex. He had sworn he would never say them in a subsequent relationship, and he had never needed to, much less wanted to. But Allegra hadn't said it, either. Somehow he had fooled himself into thinking she had, but then, he'd been wrong about that sort of thing before.

It was the same as all those years ago…

No. It was worse.

Much worse.

Back then, he'd been angry. Bitter. Furious.

Now all he felt was…*hurt*. Pain like he'd only ever experienced twice before, while staring at a coffin containing his mother and then later his father.

He had lost Allegra like he'd lost his parents. Without warning. Unexpectedly. They were there one minute and then they weren't.

Draco's chest was so tight it felt as if he was having a medical event. His throat was so raw it felt as though he'd drunk battery acid and swallowed the gear stick. Sideways. He walked to his car and got inside, gripping the steering wheel while he pulled himself together. But his thoughts keep running like a ticker tape in his pounding head.

Allegra wanted out.

She wanted him out of her life.

He was the one who was supposed to end things, not her. When he was good and ready. When it was time. She was supposed to be grateful he'd stepped in and saved her father's business and saved her from being blackmailed into bed by some sleazy creep.

Draco started the engine and backed out of the space. He had to get a handle on this. He couldn't allow someone to destroy him. Not like this. Not emotionally. He didn't do emotion. Or at least not emotion like this—the sort of emotion that pulled at every organ in his body until he couldn't draw a breath.

Fine.

He would get out of her life. What had he been thinking, trying to make a marriage between them work? Their relationship was doomed to fail and he was a fool for thinking he could pull it off.

All you had to do was say you loved her.

Draco braked on the thought. He didn't love Allegra. He hadn't fallen in love since he was nineteen and he wasn't going to do it now. He no longer had the 'falling in love' gene. Caring was his thing instead. He was damn good at it too. Look at the way Yanni was improving. Look at what he had done for Iona. Look at the way he provided for his staff all over the globe.

If Allegra couldn't settle for being cared about, then it was her problem, not his. So, he was alone again? He could deal with it. Would have to deal with it. He wasn't going to pay lip service to a concept he no longer believed in.

If he ever had.

Allegra wasn't sure how the press found out about her break-up with Draco but the newsfeeds were running hot by the end of the weekend. There was speculation on who was to blame for the split and she felt uncomfortable that most people assumed it was Draco. It seemed a little unfair although, given his 'playboy' track record and her quiet nun-like existence, it was an easy assumption to make. But it didn't sit well with her sense of justice.

Her father called and threatened to disinherit her for acting as lawyer to Elena but she'd simply hung up on him and blocked his number.

Emily called around to her house late on Sunday night with chocolates, wine and a shoulder to cry on. 'Are you sure you're doing the right thing, Allegra? I mean, it's only been a couple of weeks. Lots of marriages hit rough spots in the early days.'

'I had to leave him,' Allegra said. 'He doesn't love me. It's a deal breaker for me.'

'But some men are hopeless at admitting to loving someone,' Emily said. 'They literally can't say the words.'

Allegra sighed. 'I just can't bring myself to stay in a relationship that isn't equal. I love him. I think I probably always have. But he *cares* about me. That's not good enough. I want him to love me like I love him.'

Emily snapped off a big chunk of fruit and nut chocolate, ignoring the wine she had poured earlier. 'I don't know… I can't help feeling you're making a big mistake. But who am I to talk?'

'So, still no word from Loukas?'

Emily's shoulders drooped. 'Nope.' She eyed the chocolate in her hand for a moment then made a funny gurgling noise and dropped the chocolate to cover her mouth with her hand, her face draining of colour, as though someone had tapped the blood out of her body.

'Are you okay?'

Emily bolted out of the sitting room to the nearest bathroom. Allegra followed close behind and heard her being wretchedly sick. She pushed open the door and came over to where Emily was kneeling in front of the toilet. 'Oh, you poor darling.' She reached for a face cloth and rinsed it under the tap. 'You must have caught a bug or something.'

Emily buried her face in the cloth. 'Yeah, or something…' She came out from behind the face cloth and grimaced. 'You think you've got problems. Wait till you hear mine.'

Allegra frowned. 'You're not…?'

'I haven't done the test yet,' Emily said. 'I bought one—actually, I bought a couple—but I'm not game to do it. I keep hoping I'll get my period. I'm never late. I've never been even a day late. You could set Big Ben by me normally.' Her chin began to tremble. 'What if I'm pregnant? What am I going to do?'

'You'll have to tell Loukas. I assume he's the…?'

'Yes…'

'Are you going to keep—?'

'Yes.' Emily's expression had a look about it of a lioness protecting its cub. She even placed her hand over her flat abdomen. 'Of course I'm keeping it.'

'You'll have to tell Loukas.'

Emily scraped her hair back off her face. 'Yeah, really looking forward to that.' She gave a rueful twist of her mouth. 'You and I are a pair, aren't we?'

Tell me about it.

A few days later, Draco received a package in the post of Allegra's rings and the pendant he'd given her. There was a short handwritten note expressing her concern that he was getting the blame for their break-up.

But you are to blame.

He freeze-framed the thought. The last few days had been some of the most miserable of his existence. It was like reliving the grief of losing his mother and father. The unexpectedness of it. The blunt shock. The *how the hell do I cope with this*? The pointless 'what if?'s and '*what could I have done to prevent this from happening?*'.

Draco couldn't stay in his house with those gifts staring at him. They were the symbols of his failure. He walked out to the street but everywhere he looked he was reminded of what he had lost. Couples were walking hand in hand along the river. Families were picnicking on the lush grass, children playing and laughing in the summer sunshine. He saw a young father scoop a giggling toddler off the grass and hold her against him with a proud smile at her cuteness. His young pregnant wife came over and slipped her arm through her partner's, and beamed up at him with such affection it made Draco's chest tighten.

This was what Allegra wanted. Connection. Love. A family.

Didn't he want it too? Deep, deep inside was a locked compartment of his personality that secretly ached for what that young couple had. His parents had had it but it had been snatched away with his mother's early death. His father had done his best—more than his best—to provide a happy family life, but the threat of loss had hung over Draco and his father, until finally it delivered its felling blow.

Draco had shied away from loving people since because he always lost them. His mother, his father, his ex. Even his boss and mentor Josef had died soon after selling him the business. He had closed off his heart to protect himself from further loss, yet, by doing so, he had lost the person most important to him.

He had lost Allegra.

But, unlike with his mother and father, Draco could fix this.

He loved her.

Really loved her. Not just cared about her. But loved her with every cell of his being. Why else had he all but frogmarched her into marriage? He had married her before anyone else could because he loved her too much to see her suffer with a man who wouldn't respect and treasure her the way he would. His streak of protectiveness was a cover-up for love.

Everything he felt about her was real. Real love. Love that lived, breathed and blossomed for a lifetime. The sort of love he'd been too frightened to own because he didn't want to lose it. Like he had lost it when his gold-digger girlfriend had decided she wanted someone richer than him. But what he'd felt for that girl was nothing to what he felt for Allegra. He had blocked his feelings for so long, but they were seeping through the armour around his heart until it was all but bursting out of his chest.

It was time to fess up and win back the girl of his dreams. The love of his life.

Yes, that was exactly was what Allegra was—*his life*.

Allegra got home late after a mediation meeting ran over time and still the husband refused to settle. She thought longingly of that week, sailing around the Greek islands with Draco, when dirty divorces were the last thing on her mind. Not a minute went past without her thinking of him, wondering how soon he would find someone else once their marriage was formally over. She could have drawn up the papers herself, or got one of her colleagues to do it, but her heart wasn't in it. She would leave it to him to sort out. He was the one who'd wanted the marriage in the first place. It was his mess to undo.

She had only just got inside and slipped off her coat and heels when the doorbell rang. Something about how the bell rang made her pulse pick up its pace. Emily did a quick 'one-two' buzz. Her neighbour on the left held it down for three counts and the neighbour on the right used the brass door-knocker instead.

This sounded…urgent. Insistent. 'I'm not going away until you answer' insistent.

Allegra peered through the peephole and her heart did a backflip as good as any Olympic gymnast. She opened the door with a hand that felt more like an empty glove than a hand. 'Draco...'

'May I come in?'

She held open the door. 'Of course.' Allegra closed the door and turned to face him. 'Did you get the package with...? Oh, you've brought it with you.'

Draco placed the package on the hall table and turned to face her again. 'You didn't actually say you loved me the other day.'

Allegra licked her suddenly dry lips. 'I... No. I didn't see the point since—'

'Then let me be the first to say it.' He took her by the upper arms in a gentle grip, his dark, lustrous eyes meshing with hers. 'I love you.'

For a moment she just looked at him, completely stunned. She had longed to hear those words for so long and now she'd heard them she was too overcome with emotion to speak. She gazed into his eyes, her heart thumping so erratically, as if it was looking for an exit route out of her chest. 'You're not just saying it to get me to come back to you?'

His hands tightened as if he was worried she was going to slip out of his grasp. 'I'm saying it because it's true. I love you so much it, scared me to admit it. I've been a fool, Allegra. A stubborn, block-headed fool. Can you ever forgive me for putting you through the last few days? If you've felt even a quarter of the despair I've felt then I deserve to be horsewhipped.'

She touched his face, not sure if this was really happening.

He loved her. Draco loved her.

'I love you too. I think I may have done so since I was sixteen. But it's grown from a silly crush to love of such depth and intensity, I can hardly describe it. I just know I feel it and I can't imagine ever not feeling it.'

He smiled and hugged her close, rocking her against him as if he wanted them to be glued together. 'I'm sorry for the other night. I was blindsided by your decision to end things. I didn't see it coming because I was too proud to admit you had the raw end of the deal.' Draco eased back to look down at her. 'I've got a lot to learn about giving and taking in a relationship, but I hope you'll teach me. If you've got the patience, that is.'

Allegra pressed a kiss to his mouth, breathing in the familiar scent of him that thrilled her senses so much. 'Maybe you could teach me to be a little less insecure. I've been torturing myself with images of you taking up with someone else.'

'There is no one else for me, *agape mou*,' Draco said. 'I realised that during my epiphany earlier this evening. I made those promises when we got married because there could never be anyone else for me. My subconscious must have known it, even if I wasn't ready to admit it. I told myself I was marrying you to protect you, but what was motivating that protectiveness was love. You are my heart. My life. Can we start again? Stay married and live together for the rest of our lives, in a partnership others will envy and want to emulate?'

Allegra hugged him so tightly her arms ached. 'I can think of nothing I'd like better.'

'I wish I'd gone about this differently,' he said. 'It would have saved these last days of hell.'

'They were hell for me too,' she said. 'But that's all behind us now.'

A shadow passed through his gaze. 'I couldn't be in

my house after you sent back the gifts I'd given you. It was like coming back to the house after my parents' funerals. Even though they died years apart, the feelings were exactly the same. Seeing stuff sitting there but knowing they were never coming back to collect it. It's the worst feeling in the world. The sense of helplessness. Aloneness. Emptiness. That's when I realised I had blocked my feelings out of fear. I didn't want to lose you, like I'd lost everyone else I cared about, so I fooled myself into thinking I didn't love you. But then I realised why I was feeling so bad. Not out of pride or because of the business arrangement. But because my life is meaningless without you in it.'

Allegra stroked a fingertip around his mouth. 'I was so miserable after you left. I couldn't understand why you weren't fighting to keep our marriage. It sort of confirmed my doubts in a way. But now I realise how hard it must have been for you, with me springing it on you like that. I just couldn't go another day without knowing for sure how you felt.'

'I should have fought for you. But I guess I was feeling so raw I had to get away to process things. But it's not going to be how I solve conflict in the future.'

His eyes looked suspiciously watery. 'I saw a family today. A young family with a toddler, and the wife was expecting another baby. It made me realise what I was missing out on. I don't want to be surrounded by my wealth and possessions at the end of my life. I want to be surrounded by my family. *Our* family.'

She framed his face in her hands. 'You say you've been denying how you feel about me—well, I've been denying how I feel about having kids. I've suppressed my maternal longings for years as I worked to build my career. I don't want to get to the end of my life with a stack of legal documents for company. I want you. I want us to be family. And I want to live in Greece. It's my home. I want to set up a legal practice where I can help women like Iona and Elena. Iona might fancy a career change as a nanny. I'm going to ask her next time I see her. If ever there was a frustrated grand-mother, she's one.'

His smile lit up his eyes, making them crinkle at the corners. 'That's been my mistake in the past—think-ing "either, or" instead of both. We can both have what we want. It will take a bit of compromise on my part, but you're going to give me lessons, *ne*?'

Allegra gave him a teasing smile. 'When would you like me to start?'

He brought his mouth down to within a millimetre of hers. 'After I do this.' And he covered her mouth with his.

* * * * *

If you enjoyed
WEDDING NIGHT WITH HER ENEMY,
why not explore these other
WEDLOCKED! titles?

BOUND BY HIS DESERT DIAMOND
by Andie Brock
BRIDE BY ROYAL DECREE
by Caitlin Crews
CLAIMED FOR THE DE CARRILLO TWINS
by Abby Green
THE DESERT KING'S CAPTIVE BRIDE
by Annie West
THE SHEIKH'S BOUGHT WIFE
by Sharon Kendrick

Available now!

MILLS & BOON®

MODERN™

POWER, PASSION AND IRRESISTIBLE TEMPTATION

Join Britain's BIGGEST Romance Book Club

- **EXCLUSIVE offers** every month

- **FREE delivery direct** to your door

- **NEVER MISS a title**

- **EARN Bonus Book** points

Call Customer Services
0844 844 1358*

or visit
millsandboon.co.uk/subscriptions

* This call will cost you 7 pence per minute plus your phone company's price per minute access charge.